the truth about rats, rules, & seventh grade

the truth about rats, rules, & seventh grade

by: Linda Zinnen

HarperCollinsPublishers

The Truth about Rats, Rules, & Seventh Grade

Printed in the United States of America. For information address HarperCollins Children's Books, a division of HarperCollins Publishers,
1350 Avenue of the Americas, New York, NY 10019.
www.harperchildrens.com

Library of Congress Cataloging-in-Publication Data
Zinnen, Linda.
The truth about rats, rules, & seventh grade / Linda Zinnen.
p. cm.
Summary: Eleven-year-old Larch has depended on her own rules to help her cope with the life she and her mother share in a trailer in a small Ohio town, but her rules do not help her deal with a rat-catching dog, her best friend's crush, and the truth she learns about her father's death.
ISBN 0-06-028799-3 — ISBN 0-06-028800-0 (lib. bdg.)
[1. Mothers and daughters—Fiction. 2. Schools—Fiction.
3. Dogs—Fiction. 4. Ohio—Fiction.] I. Title.
PZ7.Z6545 Tr 2001 00-27126
[Fic]—dc21

Typography by Fumi Kosaka
1 2 3 4 5 6 7 8 9 10
❖
First Edition

For my mother and father,

who speak the truth in love

the truth

about rats, rules, & seventh grade

Chapter One

My school was a dump.

It had asbestos ceiling tiles, lead pipes, and about a hundred layers of chalk dust floating through the air—one for every year Pottsville Grammar had been in business. None of the third-story windows opened more than three inches. Fall and winter, the radiators clanked and hissed right through Wednesday afternoons, when the inside temperature got up to maybe sixty-five degrees. Then they knocked off for the weekend. That pretty gray slate roof with the greeny-gold copper gutters? Leaked like a bandit. The drips got so bad in the third-grade classroom, the bucket rusted to the floor and the little kids had to use a margarine tub to bail it out every day during the month of April.

And then there was that whole thing with Mrs. Hogstettler.

Until last year, Mrs. Hogstettler's seventh-grade class ran like it always had. Handouts on the Dewey decimal system. African geography straight off a map featuring the Belgian Congo. Desks in rows. Lots of yelling. Kids trading Hog jokes during recess.

What do you get when you cross
the Hog with a black belt in
karate?
Pork chops.

But last year—the year I was in seventh grade, the year my class was gonna be the one thinking up Hog jokes—suddenly she said we could call her Mrs. Marilyn. First day of school we pushed our desks together and formed Learning Teams. By mid-October, we had done Team Units on Space Exploration, Helen Keller, and The Native American. Every afternoon Mrs. Marilyn plugged one nostril and took deep cleansing breaths during Sustained Silent Reading.

"She's going through the change of life," my friend MaryEllen said. "And she is taking us with her."

What next?

"Gang—" chirped Mrs. Marilyn.

I frowned. Teachers never used to call their students "gang."

"Gang, this November marks the one hundred sixty-eighth anniversary of Pottsville's founding."

"Big deal," said Tom Prouty. Tom sat catty-corner from me on my Learning Team. Let me tell you, having Tom Prouty on your Learning Team is a gigantic detour on the road to an Education.

"Pottsville, of course," continued Mrs. Marilyn, "is one of the most important towns of southeast-central rural Ohio. Why, we sit at the edge of the coalfields, in the cusp of the foothills, on the verge of fertile farmlands—"

"—by the bend of a river," chanted the class. "Pottsville, the crossroads of southeast-central o-HI-o."

"Big deal," said Tom Prouty again.

"Now," said Mrs. Marilyn, "the Pottsville Boosters have declared the second Saturday in November Founder's Day. And we have been asked"—Mrs. Marilyn paused dramatically—"to write and illustrate a book. *Who's Who of Pottsville, Ohio.*"

I kicked Tom fiercely.

"Ow, Larch!"

"Do not say 'big deal' one more time," I whispered. "Do not."

"As soon as the Boosters asked me, I wrote

an Ohio Department of Education grant application for a computer and multimedia package. I thought this was surely the project that would finally bring in the funding for a school computer, but . . ." Mrs. Marilyn shrugged and held up a Wal-Mart bag.

"The grant was enough money for a three-ring binder and a couple of disposable cameras. We can take a snapshot of each person we profile and paste them in the book." Mrs. Marilyn looked distastefully at the cameras. "Maybe a photo montage or something?"

"Yeah, *cool*!" shouted Tom. "Photo whaddayacallits. We can cut up the pictures and write speech bubbles coming out of their mouths, like they're talkin' to each other and stuff."

Mrs. Marilyn swallowed hard and smiled. "That's the spirit, Tom," she said.

Tom smirked and kicked me back.

Mrs. Marilyn took a quick, cleansing breath that sounded an awful lot like a sigh. She put away the Wal-Mart bag. Next thing, we were discussing biography's form and function. I opened my notebook and headed a clean, blank page

Biography

and drew a line down the middle of my paper. A column for *Form*. A column for *Function*. Two orderly rows, two neat lists. This is how my mind works.

I like school. I am way good at it. In fact, I skipped fourth grade. I found out later that you're not supposed to skip fourth grade. Kindergarten would have been okay, and maybe second grade, but by fourth, the kids are all in cliques, and skipping is real hard on the skipper's social growth. Plus, she misses a chunk of multiplication facts and the area of a triangle and stuff, which could mess up her college plans.

But it worked out okay. MaryEllen Stillwater, my best friend, is a year older than me. I ended up in fifth grade with her. And I already knew the times tables.

While Mrs. Marilyn talked, she passed around a coffee can filled with folded slips of paper. Everybody took one.

"On each paper is the name of a prominent Pottsville citizen," she said.

"Awrright!" yelled Tom. "I got Jessie Stanton, the eighth-grade homecoming queen!" Mrs. Marilyn gave him a look.

"After a few expository paragraphs detailing the basic facts—middle name, birthdate, education, family ties, and so forth—I want you to summarize in clear and meaningful language the guiding principles of your *Who's* life."

I frowned. Teachers didn't used to discuss Guiding Principles. They whacked us around with The Rules instead.

"For instance," said Mrs. Marilyn, "I asked my oldest son, Robbie, what he thought my guiding principle as his mother had been. Robbie said,

'Kick Butt and Take Names.'"

I frowned harder. Teachers never used to say "Kick Butt."

"Your guiding principle, Tom, seems to be God Grant Me the Strength to Be Obnoxious," observed Mrs. M.

I snickered. "Teacher called you obnoxious," I whispered. Tom stuck out his tongue. I stuck out mine back.

Mrs. Marilyn patted MaryEllen's shoulder. "Yours must be Is Everybody Happy Yet?"

Boy. Isn't that the truth? MaryEllen is my best friend and a dear, sweet, gentle pushover.

"How about you, Larch?" asked Mrs. Marilyn. "What's your guiding principle?"

"Stuck-Up and Stupid," hissed Tom. "Ow, Larch!"

I stood up, threw back my shoulders, and answered proudly, "My number one guiding principle is: The Rules Are the Rules." I glared at Tom.

The dismissal bell rang. The class let out a whoop and headed for the doors.

I looked at my *Who's Who* name from the coffee can. Ezra Fenton, township trustee. Hmmm. I knew Mr. Fenton. Hard to imagine him being guided by principles, exactly. He was pretty cranky.

I stuffed Mr. Fenton in my history book and turned toward the door. Susanna Gibson was talking to Mrs. Marilyn.

". . . so if I could? Switch? It'd be easier, you know?" Susanna handed her *Who's Who* paper to Mrs. Marilyn. Mrs. M. read it and called me over.

"Larch, would you switch your *Who* with Susanna? You live just across the field from school, and since he's here only Tuesdays, Thursdays, and every other Friday evening . . ."

Susanna grabbed Mr. Fenton by the corner and yanked him loose. "Gee, Larch? I, like, don't even care? Who it is? Thanks, huh?"

Mrs. Marilyn handed me Susanna's paper. I read it and frowned.

Charles Randall Prouty, school janitor. Tom Prouty's dad.

What next?

Chapter Two

Tom Prouty is drop-dead gorgeous.

He has this thick, black hair and pea-green eyes and a lazy smile with a dimple in his left cheek. He is tall and rangy and excellent at baseball. His voice is husky and slow. Hmmm. Am I the kind of girl who covers up her true feelings for a boy by pretending to feel nothing but disdain?

Nope. Tom Prouty is drop-dead gorgeous, all right. A drop-dead gorgeous jerk.

Like my mom. Mom is gorgeous too (she's not a jerk), gorgeous in a different way than Tom: auburn hair and hazel eyes, one or two dramatic freckles, no dimple. She has a great figure, even though she works at the Duke of Donuts full-time and buys all this junk food for the microwave.

Only thing is, Mom smokes and smokes.

I look like my mom—but like I went through the wash cycle where the *gorgeous* washed out and everything else faded to carrots and pale brown, except for half a million chocolate freckles all over my body. However, I do not and never will smoke.

Well. The same day I got stuck writing about Tom Prouty's dad, Mom nuked a bunch of pancakes for supper. She lit a cigarette and asked me what was up for homework. I told her about *Who's Who*.

"And you got Chuck Prouty? He's a nice guy. I talked with him once or twice after your dad died."

I laid my fork in my plate and studied the syrup patterns.

I talked with him once or twice after your . . .

It caught me off balance. Those couple of

words were the most Mom had said to me in the last nine years about the car wreck. Not like she'd ever been a big talker. But she told me once about how my dad died in a car crash when I was two years old. See? I knew the facts. I knew all about it.

But this was different, personal, about Mom. I didn't want her to notice how hard I was listening—she stopped talking if she thought I was really listening—so I said, "Boy, you dated Chuck Prouty? But he's married and has all those stupid kids."

I glanced casually out the kitchen window. Beyond a brushy windbreak lay the empty field between the school and our trailer lot. I could see Mr. Prouty's beat-up Chev parked under the school's basketball hoop.

"I didn't *date* him, Larch." Mom yawned. She pushed around a couple of dead butts in the ashtray with the tip of her lit cigarette. "We talked a few times after church is all. He and Beth invited me over for supper once, I think."

Okay. Mom and me had already worked this stuff out. We lived by

The Rules

1. Do not ask Elaine Mae Waysorta (mother) a direct question about her husband, Christopher Allen Waysorta (deceased).
2. Do not ask Larch Anne Waysorta (daughter) to discuss her feelings about the father (deceased), as named above.
3. Do not leave dirty underwear on the bathroom floor.

So Mom stopped talking under Rule Number 1. I was not about to get into how I had grown up around this dark, empty space called "Beats me what he was like, my daddy died before I could talk" (see Rule 2), and I knew my underwear was not in the bathroom (3).

End of conversation.

Mom yawned some more and went to bed because she had to get up at three A.M. to fry doughnuts for the Duke. MaryEllen wasn't baby-sitting, so she came over. Actually, the Stillwaters sent her over because I'm such a great example about schoolwork. MaryEllen's parents think MaryEllen doesn't apply herself and stuff.

"I hate that Tom Prouty," said MaryEllen. She was holding up a strand of her long brown hair and picking at the split ends. "Don't you hate that Tom Prouty?"

"Tom Prouty is a jerk," I said, writing. I didn't look up from the English assignment. "He never hands in his part of group projects on time. He spells like a third grader. When he yawns—which is constantly—spit hangs off his molars. You're lucky you don't have him on your Learning Team."

"He's gonna write about Jessie Stanton,"

MaryEllen murmured into her split ends. "He'll never look at a seventh-grade girl after that."

I put down my pen. "Wait a minute. I'm getting that you *like* Tom."

MaryEllen thumped her head down on her pile of books and moaned into her homework. "You don't understand, Larch! *I* don't understand! It just *is*. The way I *feel*."

I frowned. "Think about it, MaryEllen. How can you like a boy that in ten years is going to be holding down a full-time job at the Gas 'n' Save?"

"This isn't a head thing, Larch," she mumbled. "This is a heart thing."

I frowned harder. "Well okay, a heart thing, I guess I can understand that. But Tom Prouty? What a loser!"

"You think?"

I waved my hands impatiently. "They're all losers. When I look around our class and think, 'Well, here's what we'll be dragging to the high school prom,' honestly, I get sick to my stomach."

"But—"

"Think college, MaryEllen."

"But—"

"Think graduate school."

"But—"

"Think about the whole world!"

"I kind of like Pottsville," said MaryEllen softly. "It's pretty in the fall."

I picked up my pen. "Yeah. And a dump the rest of the time."

MaryEllen moaned a little more and then went home. I finished my homework, fished an apple out of the back of the fridge, and turned on the TV.

I don't watch a lot of TV, but I'd gotten into the habit of watching this program called *Fitz*. It sort of spoke to my life. Susanna Gibson told me about it.

"It's about this handsome guy?" she said. "From Boston and his family's really rich and everything? So Fitz graduated from Harvard Law

School, and like, every week he struggles to find the meaning of life? Working? For this big-deal law firm? In New York City?"

Susanna went on and on about Fitz. Basically, Fitz is just another handsome jerk. But. He has this girlfriend named Lauren who works in publishing. And Lauren has the most gorgeous bathroom I have ever seen.

Her bathroom is sea green and gray. It has a skylight and hanging plants and a terra cotta tile floor. It has this combination Jacuzzi-hot tub-shower-sauna thing that looks like it could fly to the moon. Every show has at least one scene in Lauren's bathroom. Lauren puts on makeup and takes off makeup and comes out of the shower and goes into the shower. That week she caught Fitz kissing her next-apartment neighbor in her bathroom, right next to the heated towel bars.

I snorted. What next?

The bathroom in our house trailer is about as different from Lauren's as it could get. The entire bathroom is the size of Lauren's built-in oak towel cupboard. Our bathroom has orange indoor-outdoor carpet, fluorescent lights, and a scummy shower curtain. The toilet seat is cracked. Mom swears she's gonna buy a new one, but she never does. Mold has turned the grouting black. Once a week I get down on my hands and knees and scrub every single inch of the bathroom with Lysol. Doesn't matter. The whole place smells like mildew.

But watching old Fitz make a jerk out of himself in Lauren's bathroom, I thought about it some. When I had it made, I would have a bathroom like Lauren's wonder. Larch's wonder. I would sink down into the hot tub–launching pad with my glass of wine balanced on the pure white grout next to my mega-RAM laptop and listen to the towel bars overheat. I would stare through the skylight at the starry night sky. I would never struggle with the meaning of my life in the bathroom. Growing up in Pottsville—growing up with no daddy and a *real* quiet mom, stuck in a dead-end school that couldn't afford just one lousy computer—boy. My life already had *loads* of meaning.

I thought about our cracked toilet seat. I wondered what Lauren's looked like, her toilet. They never showed it on TV.

Chapter Three

My *Who's Who* project turned into a disaster.

Two weeks went by. I didn't interview Mr. Prouty. Every time I thought about Mom talking to Mr. Prouty about the car wreck all those years ago, I got stuck. I didn't know why. Though sitting across from Tom Prouty's stupid self every day didn't help much. The thought of getting to know the father of the family made me gag.

Friday afternoon came. I knew I had to start right away in order to do my usual three careful drafts and still hand it in a couple of days early. Mr. Prouty didn't clean the school until Fridays late, so I went home and hung around for a while until I saw him circle his Chev under the basketball hoop.

I stepped through the windbreak and cut across the school's empty field. It was already way past five; the sunset had turned evening gold. My sneakers crunched over the flattened grass.

When I was in first grade, a bunch of us used to play soccer in this field during lunch recess. One real hot spring day, when her team had been losing bad, MaryEllen said, "Hey. Let's get a drink at your house, Larch."

"No," I said. "There's a drinking fountain at school."

"But, Larch, I'm thirsty right here, and we're about sitting on your front steps!"

"It's school. We have to use the drinking fountain."

"She don't have a key to get in anyway," said someone.

"Do so," I said.

"No you don't."

I pulled out my door key tied to a piece of yarn around my neck. "Do so."

"*Oooooooooo*, her mom got her a key!"

"You are so lucky, Larch!"

"What's the point of having a key if we don't get any grape juice?" asked MaryEllen.

I was just a little bitty kid, but I already knew the answer. "Rules are rules, MaryEllen."

I had lived in the trailer park next to the school's empty field all my life, and until that moment walking across the grass, I had never been on school property past four o'clock. I had never thrown a ball at the gym windows, called somebody a cootie head, or talked during a fire drill. Rules are rules.

The school's south door was unlocked. Even though I was there on official *Who's Who* business, the idea of going inside after hours made me stand for a minute flipping my *Who* notebook open and shut to calm myself. Finally, I pushed the door open.

"Mr. Prouty?" I shouted. My voice boomed down the hallway.

School sure was strange. With the overhead lights off and the classroom doors shut, I walked down the first floor hall in total, hand-in-front-of-my-face darkness. I stumbled past the primary classrooms. Miss Robe had left her door open a little. A million yellow sun motes filtered into the hallway from her west-facing windows: a lemon-pie slice of sunset.

The quiet was strange, too. During school when everybody's on recess, the hall is quiet because all the noise is outside. This new kind of quiet—quiet inside, quiet outside—was cold and empty and hollow and sad.

I admit, I was kind of spooked.

"Hey, Mr. Prouty?" I called up the stairs.

I was halfway up the stairs to the second floor

when I heard it. *Rhist, rhist, rhist*. Something was dragging across the floor above my head. I froze on the stairs.

There was breathing. Silent breathing—about two feet off the floor. It sounded like snake breathing. Python breathing.

"M-M-Mr. Prouty?" I whispered. I had a double-handed death grip on the banister.

Whee-eeze, ma-whee-eeze. Snake breath whistled down the stairs above my head.

Bravely, I looked up. In the faint light thrown by the hallway window, I could see a halo of scruffy fur atop four bony legs. A whiskery snout poked through the railings and sniffed the air. I frowned. Maybe the goat had swallowed the python instead of the other way around.

Without letting go of the banister, I craned my neck for a better look. The python growled at me. I shot my head back down.

"You're not a python, you're a dog," I said, totally relieved.

Now that I had gotten a good look at him, I could see he was just a plain old mangy rat terrier. Sparse, coarse fur dotted with liver spots. A barrel-shaped body, skinny shinbones, muzzle like a pig snout.

"You're pretty ugly for a dog, pal. You'd do better as a python," I said.

The dog drew back, offended. He turned and padded out of sight. By the time I ran up the stairs, the dog's tail was disappearing down the staircase at the other end of the hall.

Well. There were rules against dogs in school. When I caught up with him, I'd boot him out of the building.

That dog padded down three flights of stairs straight to the basement. I caught up with him as he trotted into the furnace room.

Smart, smart dog. If you were a stray caught trespassing, and someone—who was kind of trespassing herself—was going to boot your skinny shanks out into the parking lot, where better to hide than the dim, creepy basement? The furnace room especially, which had a big blue sign posted on the door: POSITIVELY NO STUDENTS ALLOWED IN FURNACE ROOM AT ANY TIME.

I stood outside the furnace room and looked up and down the corridor. Maybe Mr. Prouty would show up. I stood around some more. He didn't.

Inside the furnace room the dog was rustling around, obviously making himself at home. That did it. The sooner he was out, the better.

The furnace room was lit with fluorescent lights, bright as day. It was so bright, I had to shut my eyes a minute to adjust. With my eyes out of the picture, the first thing that hit me was

The Furnace Room Smell

1. Steal Tom Prouty's gym socks, the ones he hasn't changed since Labor Day.
2. Put a rotten egg in one sock. Not a slimy just-gone-rotten egg, but

one that's been mummified by years of coal-fired boiler heat—ash hot and choking, mixed with a whiff of boiled-dry radiator paint.

3. Wrap the egg-sock around your nose.
4. Inhale deeply.

I bent over and pinched my nose shut. Tears leaked out of my eyes.

"Pee-yew," I said. The rustling stopped.

When I thought I could take it, I stood up straight and took my fingers away from my nose. The dog poked his blunt head around the far boiler and snarled at me.

I chased him around the boilers. He scooted behind a huge pile of broken desks and chairs. I climbed the desks.

I had a clear view of the corner the dog had staked out. He had dragged over a dirty green blanket. Nearby was a bowl of water and a plate full of dog kibble. Hmmm. Water and dog food? Was someone feeding that dog?

"What are you doing?" asked Mr. Prouty behind me. Now, Mr. Prouty is a tall man and his voice boomed straight in my ear. Boy, I jumped. I turned around fast—too fast. The pile shifted under my feet and I slid right off the topmost desk.

Mr. Prouty grabbed my arm on the way down. "Hey! You're gonna kill yourself."

When I had both feet back on the concrete floor, he squinted at me and remarked, "Larch, you are about the last student I'd expect to see down here breaking the rules."

"Well, I sure didn't plan to," I said.

I told him about the *Who's Who* stuff and ended with, "But first there's a stray dog down here we need to turn out."

"Him? Yeah, he's a stray, all right, but he ain't no slacker. These foundations are chock full of holes and all the little field rats are just pourin' in the building now, looking for a winter home. Dog's the best ratter I've ever seen."

I shuddered. "He was sniffing around on the second floor. You . . . you don't think a rat got up there, do you?"

"Maybe."

"Mrs. Marilyn's room is on the second floor!" I peered through the tangle of chair legs and whistled. "Here doggie, good doggie. Let's go back upstairs, okay, doggie?"

Mr. Prouty folded his arms and watched me here-doggie-doggie. "He's gone. He's got his own bolt hole back there. Dog's been here a month and far as I know, nobody but you and me have seen him." He sat behind his janitor's desk next to the boiler. "He don't like children much."

"Yeah, he growled at me. Twice." I pulled a folding chair over to the other side of the desk and sat down. On the boiler right above Mr. Prouty's head was a big yellow sticker:

CAUTION
ASBESTOS
Do not handle without
proper training and equipment.

Well. I opened my *Who* notebook and a very weird thing happened. When I looked down at Question Number One, all I saw was Mom's cigarette playing around in the ashtray—

I talked with him once or twice after your dad died.

—and I had this vision of Mom and her cigarette standing outside a big, dark, empty space, where she's holding up a flashlight and waving me over the threshold, and past the dark is my dad, it's my dad, except the flashlight's got dead batteries and Mom's not waving me through at all. She's pushing me away.

"Why? Why's she doing that?" I blurted out.

"What?" asked Mr. Prouty.

My eyes closed in embarrassment. But not my mouth. Boy, my mouth kept going.

"Dad died nine years ago," explained Mouth. "His car smashed into a tree. He wasn't drunk, but the car was going too fast and he wasn't wearing a seat belt. I don't miss him. I don't. How can you miss somebody who died before you could even talk? But my mom—" Mouth clamped shut.

But my mom. We didn't have one single picture of her since that car wreck. Not one personal letter. Our house didn't have one single hand-knit afghan to curl up in, or a book turned face-down on the arm of the couch, or knickknacks that sat around and collected dust. Only things on our calendar were her work days and what I penciled in. Project due. Return library book. School bake sale.

I opened my eyes and smoothed the notebook page. *Favorite color. Favorite food. Favorite song when you were eleven. Favorite guiding principle.* I had worked hard on these questions to ask Charles Randall Prouty. In half an hour, I'd know all this stuff about him. Stuff I didn't know about my dad. Stuff I didn't know about my mom, even.

"Mom talked to you a couple times, huh," I said softly. "When she used to go to church."

Mr. Prouty rubbed his chin. It was plain he was as surprised as I was about all this.

"Wait a minute, Larch," he kept saying. "Larch, wait a minute." He moved some papers around the top of his desk and rubbed his chin some more.

"Yeah, I guess we talked a little right after the accident," he said, finally. "We haven't talked but to say 'hello' for years, so I don't know. Your mama was so stricken back then, not a scratch on her, not even a bruise, and she couldn't get over—"

I felt hot, dizzy. "She was in the car?"

"She was driving," Mr. Prouty said absentmindedly, a split second before he realized he was giving me a real news flash. "You didn't know that? She never told you she was driving?"

"Nope," I whispered, "nope." I closed my eyes and put my head between my knees because I was going to throw up and it already stunk bad enough in there.

"Mom never told me how she killed my dad," I said faintly.

Mr. Prouty leaned across the desk and jerked me upright by the collar. He shook me hard.

"Don't you *say* that crap. Don't you *think* that crap. That *tree* killed your dad. It was an *accident*," he roared.

I brushed off his fingers and picked up my notebook. "I'm gonna go home now," I said. My voice hardly wavered. "I'm gonna go."

"Wait a minute, Larch," said Mr. Prouty. "Larch, wait a minute!"

I didn't wait a minute. I also didn't go home. I walked all over Pottsville in the dark, trying to get a grip. My mind went over and over and over

<u>The Crash</u>

1. Down the stairs.
2. In the car. Dad tosses the keys to

Mom and says, "You drive." Why not, women drive all the time, right?

3. Past the school, turn left, turn left again.
4. Straight onto Route 62, speed up, cars turning; Mom fiddles with the radio, glances at him, and says, "Okay?"
5. Over the Folson Hill Bridge that the Highway Department paints a pretty sky blue; radio's a little too loud, car's going a little too fast, road's a little too slippery.
6. Hit the bridge embankment.
7. And crash.

   (A) Into a tree—that big, solid hundred-year-old oak growing right where the bridge ends.

   (B) Branches smash the windshield. Glass flies everywhere.

See? My mind got it. It got what Mr. Prouty was saying. I had drawn a neat line down the middle, headed one column *Accident*, and listed all the things that might have happened: A sneeze, a laugh, a yawn. A dog running across the road. A newspaper blown on the windshield. A southbound car swerving into the northbound lane. A wind gust. Sun glare. Darkness. Rain. Fog.

Then there was the other column.

The other column, *Non-Accident*, had a few little things listed, too. Like: Driving under the Influence of Drugs or Alcohol. Intent to Harm. Conspiracy to Collect Dad's Life Insurance Policy (given how we scraped by, I crossed that one off). Vehicular Homicide. Manslaughter. Murder.

As my mind went over and over it, that mixed-up feeling I had about my dad drifted like the cigarette smoke across my mother's stone-cold face. I suddenly got why she hardly went anywhere but to the Duke at three A.M. Because she was hard. And why we didn't have any

Waysorta keepsakes lying around. Because she was cruel. Why she slept all the time and smoked all the time and never said much of anything to me. Because she was guilty.

See? My mind got that, too. My mother killed my father.

Chapter Four

When I got back to the trailer, it was late, Mom was asleep, and I had

<u>The Truth</u>

1. My dad was dead because my mom wrecked the car.
2. My mom never told me.
3. I had to learn this the hard way, from a complete stranger with the last name of Prouty.

<u>With One Question</u>

1. Why?

I couldn't answer that. My brain was churning. I had to stop thinking for a minute. I had to stop the car that crashed again and again in my head and stop the rage that boiled over in my heart every time that car smashed that tree—calm down, I told myself—I had to freeze my blood and soul until I made it to the point where it happened—breathe deep, I told myself—a long time ago. *Not a scratch on her, not even a bruise, not a scratch not a scratch . . .*

I dragged myself into my room and lay down on the bed. My mother killed my father. My mother. Killed. My father. I rolled over and slammed my fists into the pillow. She had to pay. She had to pay and pay and pay! What if I pounded on her door, dropped to my knees at the edge of her bed—what if I shook her awake, *made* her talk . . .

But. I have never done that. Even when I got sick in the middle of the night, I would stay in bed and yell out for her.

"Mom. Mama! I feel sick."

Okay. What if I stayed put and yelled for her. She'd sit on the edge of my bed, all sleepy and groping for the cigarette in her pocket, not paying attention. Boy, would her eyes pop open when I said, "Mama. Tell me about the night you killed Daddy."

My head was throbbing. My eyes hurt. I closed them. So weird. I fell soundlessly, dreamlessly asleep.

An almighty crash woke me up. I stumbled through the hall and into the kitchen. Mom was swinging a broom and cussing loud and hard.

"There's a *rat* in here!"

My eyes popped open. Sure enough, a skinny, hairless, repulsive rat tail disappeared under the stove.

Mom froze there, panting, broom raised to the ceiling. We heard rustling. The rat was climbing around in the layers of insulation between the oven wall and the outside panels.

"Sounds like he's making a nest." My voice sounded cool, but I was shaking. Boy. There is nothing worse than a rat.

Mom dropped the broom, reached over to the stove and gently, with trembling fingers, turned on the bake setting to 500 degrees.

"We'll cook him out," she whispered.

"Why don't you turn the burners on too?" I whispered.

"I can't make myself reach over again. That . . . it . . . might jump out and bite my wrist," she whispered. "Where the veins run real close to the skin."

I shuddered, but I also thought, *Why are we whispering? Like the rat is going to understand us?* This was not rational. We were a thousand times bigger than a stupid field rat. Not to mention a thousand times smarter. I straightened up.

"I'll turn the burners on," I said loudly. And I did.

Stove heat flooded the kitchen. We sat around

for the next hour, biting our fingernails and breaking into a sweat. Quietly, we listened to the rat's contented squeaks.

"That's some good insulation in the stove," said Mom finally.

"Yeah. I guess the heat feels pretty good after freezing your tail off outdoors," I said. Bravely, I leaned over the red-hot stove and turned everything off.

"What next?" I asked.

Mom glanced at the clock. After one A.M. "We could go back to bed and hope it's gone by morning."

I considered the length of our kitchen and hallway. My bedroom door is maybe twelve feet away from the stove. The door has a two-inch gap between it and the floor. As I stood there thinking, boy, those twelve feet shrunk and the rat grew.

"I couldn't sleep," I said.

"Me neither," sighed Mom. She looked at the

stove and tapped her foot. "We could take the stove apart."

Trailer owners learn pretty quick not to put off home repairs, otherwise they roll out of bed one morning and find they can't stand up because the roof has collapsed to about shoulder level. Mom has had years of practice fixing stuff around the house. Enjoys it, too. She always cheers up when she gets out her toolbox.

"This is smart," said Mom. "This is the way to do it." She rummaged around in her toolbox and pulled out a screwdriver with an extra-long shank. "This way we won't actually have to *touch* him. When that old rat jumps out of the stove, we'll shoo him outside with the broom."

Well. We had to touch the stove. We had to pull it out from the wall and unplug it. By the time that part was done, the nerves in my hands were jumping from sharing intimate stove space with a rodent.

"Hmmm," said Mom. She squatted down and

fiddled with the stove's back panel.

She started to whistle. She tossed me a couple of flathead screws. I got a coffee mug out of the cupboard and dropped them in. My hands were still twitching. The screws tinkled musically against the bottom of the coffee mug. Mom tossed me some more. Pretty soon she had the back and one side panel propped against the refrigerator.

"Hmmm," said Mom again. She poked the screwdriver tip through the fiberglass insulation, a sheet of pink cotton candy greasy with stove crud. The rat squeaked in indignation.

"Aha!" she exclaimed, and poked harder. I jumped backward. Once that woman has a screwdriver in her hand, all caution is lost.

Suddenly a brown rat—ten feet long, three hundred pounds, easy—wriggled out of the insulation, scurried across the top of the stove, slipped down a burner hole and disappeared.

"Aha!" said Mom again. She grinned into my

panic-stricken face. "He's behind this last side panel! We got him cornered!"

Mom whaled on the last two screws. "Open the door, Larch, and stand by with the broom!"

I opened the door and cowered behind the broom.

Mom stripped the last screw and tore off the panel. The rat tried to squirm down through the fiberglass, but Mom dropped the screwdriver and with her bare hand, her *bare* hand, grabbed that rat by the base of its tail and held it up.

"Ta-dah!" she sang.

The rat's body twisted in the air. Its frantic scrabbling at her fingers got Mom's attention, all right. That brought her back to reality.

"I'm touching a *rat*!" she screeched and let go of the tail.

The rat ran wildly over the floor.

"Get it! Get it!" screamed Mom.

"*You* get it!" I screamed back. Up and down I danced, my toes determined not to touch a floor that rat feet had run over not a minute ago. The broom handle in my hand swept the flour canister off the counter. A cloud of flour exploded as the canister hit the floor.

"Hit the rat with the *broom*!" Mom yelled.

I closed my eyes against the drifting flour and brought the bristles down hard on the place where I had last seen the rat.

I swung again. The upswing caught the cupboard behind me. A jar of spaghetti sauce and a box of elbow noodles splatted to the floor. Fresh clouds of flour mushroomed on the downswing.

The rat, acting on a thousand years of rat instinct, dodged the broom, the flour canister, and the spaghetti sauce. It skittered over the noodles and darted lightning-quick into the first dark hole it found. Which happened to be the leg hole of my jeans.

Chapter Five

I dropped the broom and let out a bellow.

My jeans were too narrow at the knee, thank goodness, for the rat to slither all the way up my leg. I clapped both hands over the rat bulge at my knee and tried to push it down.

Under the denim the rat writhed and moiled between my cupped fingers like a pulsating tumor. Tickly tumor claws gripped my skin. Malignant yellow fangs scraped lightly through the fine hairs on my leg. The rat was toasty warm; leftover stove heat radiated from the wormy tail twined around my shin.

The more I pushed the rat *down*, the harder it tried to climb *up*.

I let go of my knee and screamed hideously. Mom screamed. I screamed. Mom screamed. The rat and I careened from cupboard to fridge to counter to stove, destroying everything in sight. The toaster oven crashed to the floor. The cupboard door broke a hinge. The dish drainer catapulted through the air. Forks, spoons, plates, and glasses showered all over the kitchen.

Finally, the rat let go. It dropped out of my jeans and scrabbled over my bare toes. My foot, acting on a thousand years of foot instinct, kicked straight up to the ceiling. The rat sailed through the air, hit the threshold, and scurried out of the open kitchen door. Out into the deep, dark, safe, and quiet night.

Mom slammed the door shut.

She lit a cigarette and blew out the smoke. "Whew," she said.

Our kitchen was a wreck. The stove hulked

uselessly in the middle of the floor. The door was off, the sides were off, the back dismantled. Pink fiberglass hairs and flour drifted lazily in the air currents stirred by Mom's door slam. A puke mix of chocolate-covered peanuts, spaghetti sauce, dish soap, elbow noodles, nacho chips, and hidden bits of glass smeared the linoleum from wall to wall.

"Whew," Mom said again, wearily this time. She bent over and set a kitchen chair on its feet. "It's two o'clock already. Guess I'll get ready for work."

Me, I was at the sink hoping to regain a little control. Boy, the loft that rat had achieved due to my air kick. Its rear end flew straight up in the air. The tail brushed the ceiling. Its little legs splayed wide for impact, those itty-bitty claws translucent in the overhead light, that little loathsome face twisted by the disgust that one stupid species has for another . . . I gripped the faucet, ran cold water over my face, and whimpered.

Mom put away her toolbox before she left for the Duke.

"You okay?" she asked me.

I turned off the water and dried my face. I glanced at the flour dust by my feet. Rat tracks everywhere. Here and there a wormy tail imprint. I swallowed hard. "Sure. No problem. I'm okay."

"Well. If you're sure."

"Sure I'm sure. See?" I unclenched my trembling hands and stuck them casually in my pockets.

"Okay. I'll see you at five. We'll clean up the kitchen later." She looked me over. "Did you fall asleep in your clothes? Why don't you take a shower and get cleaned up?"

She left. I whimpered. If a rat had figured out how to get into our kitchen, what was to stop it from coming back?

Bringing a pal?

And Mom thought the sensible thing to do was take off all my clothes and stand naked in the shower with *rats skittering all over the house? Was she crazy?* I was wearing these clothes until I went to college.

After a few more whimpers, I took my courage in both hands and made a dash for the living room. I turned on every single living room light and sat smack in the middle of the couch holding my jacket close to my aching stomach. When the clock hit quarter to five, boy, I was out of there, banging the screen door hard, biking like a madman for the Duke.

First time I was more than five minutes early for my paper route.

The Duke of Donuts is more than just a doughnut shop with a couple of gas pumps outside. It's the closest thing Pottsville has to a mall, and sells everything from doughnuts (duh) and groceries to fishing licenses and foam rubber pillows.

Gene King, the owner, is always trying to increase business. A couple of years ago he went in for magazines in a big way and started carrying out-of-town newspapers. Then he got a brain wave—why not organize a home delivery service?

So. I get paid ten dollars a week to deliver the *Zanesville Times-Recorder* and the *Swan County Tribune* to twenty-some houses all over town. Dr. Henderson takes the *Columbus Dispatch* and *The New York Times*. That's about as high end as it gets.

When I got to the Duke, Dora, the all-night cashier, had already heard about the rat.

"Them things is vicious," she said as she helped me fold papers.

"Dora, Larch is already upset," called Mom from the doughnut fryer.

"And dirty," continued Dora.

"Dora," called Mom again.

Dora leaned over and whispered, "And disease-carryin'."

Mom came over. "Come on. Don't rub it in."

Dora looked suffering me over. "You poor baby," she said, and off she went to the next topic.

"Now, you remind me, Elaine, to bring home a dozen eggs. My granddaughter Rachel and her Home Ec class is comin' over this morning to experiment with cake recipes. Her class is baking the cake for Founder's Day, and Rachel's got it in her head they're gonna make a gingerbread cake in the shape of the old Pottsville train depot. Why they wanta make a depot is beyond me, I know that thing's been sitting on the hill since God made dirt so it's real historical, but it's the dog pound now, for Pete's sake, you'd think they'd want something with dignity, like a nice vanilla sheet cake decorated with roses."

I stuffed the rest of the papers in my bag.

The morning was cold. I stopped in the middle of Pine Street to put on gloves that I had cut the fingertips out of so I could keep my hands warm and my aim good. Pine Street was dark and quiet; doors locked, windows shut tight. An upstairs hall light in the Tasker house shone faintly onto the street.

I rode hard trying to stay warm. If I stopped to listen, I'd hear furnaces clicking on all over town. They'd fill these old houses with the brown smell of fuel oil mixed with years of dust that had accumulated in the heating ducts. Pottsville's big frame houses, black squares against the dawn sky, shivered down to their sandstone foundations. Winter was coming. Bitter drafts and frozen pipes and icicles in the attics. Hard times for old houses.

My mind quieted, thinking about architecture. My thoughts flowed clean like the slip of my bike wheels over the wet asphalt and the *thump-siss* of the *Tribune* sliding across the Sidwells' front porch. A crow called from the top of an oak tree at the corner of Maple and Washington. The familiar shape of Bank Street Hill flattened against the white morning sky. I slung the half-empty news bag across my chest and pedaled silently on. I forgot the terrors of the night.

But what about rat fleas?

I jerked to a stop.

And disease-carryin', whispered Dora in my head. Suddenly I itched all over.

Wasn't . . . bubonic plague carried by rat fleas?

I was on the other end of town. All I had left were a couple of *T-R*'s, the *Dispatch,* and *The New York Times*. But the notion I might have rat fleas sucking my blood made me crazy. I wobbled all over the road on my bike, scratching my head, my ankles, and my neck, rocketing those *T-R*'s onto porches at warp speed. I was crazy to get home and check for fleabites.

That's how I came to throw Doc Henderson's papers straight into his Thanksgiving decorations.

"Shoot," I said. I got off my bike.

Nice old Dr. Henderson and his wife live in a low-slung, split-level, totally new brick house. MaryEllen is their granddaughter, so I've been in the house a couple of times. It is pure gorgeous. Skylights, hardwood floors, Persian carpets, a bunch of tiled bathrooms that TV Lauren could use to check her hairdo, boy. I guess the Hendersons have the most perfect house in this part of Ohio.

Every year the Hendersons pay a professional landscaping company to do seasonal displays on their front lawn. That fall the landscapers had built the frame of a small barn. Inside was sort of a barn dance thing with hay in the rafters and antique farm implements and scarecrows and stuff.

The *Dispatch* had knocked off the head of a scarecrow. I found it wedged between a hay bale and some rusty pitchforks that had big plaid bows tied to the handles. The *Times* was nowhere in sight.

I stooped to pick up the *Dispatch*. Nearby a dog barked. I brushed a couple of yards of plaid ribbon out of my face and peered toward the back of Doc's yard. At the end of his lawn was a ravine and then a hill where the huge Prouty family squeezed into a double-wide as ramshackle as ours. I couldn't see the trailer. All I could see was the huge satellite dish parked in their yard.

The Prouty dog barked again, a whiny, mangy, rat-tailed bark. Boy, Mr. Prouty sure went for ugly dogs. He took them in and taught them tricks and found out their useful (but ugly) talents and . . . hey.

"Brilliant," I told the plaid pitchforks. "I have a brilliant idea."

I threw the rest of my deliveries, rode home, glanced at the clock. Seven A.M. I called up Doc Henderson's answering machine and apologized about the missing *Times*. Then I got a package of hot dogs out of the fridge.

I needed a ratcatcher more than the school did. I had to get a good night's sleep, otherwise years would pass, I'd be a walking zombie, flunk Driver's Ed, and end up taking a curve too fast. Like Mom.

Firmly, I drew a line down the middle. A

column for *Rats*. I put up a couple of items, short and to the point. Then I had a column for *Mom*. Nothing but blank, empty space.

Focused on *Rats*, I trotted over to the school.

Have I mentioned that Pottsville Grammar was a dump? When I looked around for a terrier-sized hole in the foundation, it was obvious the dog had his pick. Some holes were big enough for a wolf, and there was one crumbling cow-sized chunk of foundation missing near the girls' bathroom. I frowned. No wonder the bathroom got so cold in the winter. And as for rat holes, forget it. I stopped counting after twenty.

"Hey dog. Here, doggie, doggie." The furnace room was under the first-grade classroom. I opened the package and took out a hot dog. The morning breeze blew fresh, enticing hot dog smell down a hole. Sure enough, a whiskery snout and two pale brown eyes appeared out of the darkness.

Convincing that dog to come to my house

took the whole package. Still, after an ugly stray dog eats ten of your hot dogs, he will act sort of friendly—in case you decide to produce more hot dogs. By the time we cut through the windbreak between our house and the school field, he was almost trotting at my heels.

Then it got weird. He refused to go in by the door. He circled our trailer until he found my bedroom window. It didn't close the last inch, and I hadn't gotten around to stuffing the crack with rags yet. He nudged under that. I frowned. That dog was so used to holes and hiding that he preferred squirming under a half-closed window to trotting over an open threshold.

Once he got in, though, he knew exactly what to do. He nosed around the rooms, growling and whining and digging with his claws. Our house trailer is held up on the corners by unmortared cinder blocks. As that dog tore up a corner of the living room carpet, a whole chorus of uneasy squeaks and rustles began to vibrate through the flooring. By the sound of it, a dozen rats had nested in the dirt crawl space under the trailer.

Home sweet home. I shuddered. Pale-faced and sweating, I leaped feetfirst onto the couch. No way was I going to have nothing but a raggy piece of carpet and a sheet of pressboard between me and rat pandemonium.

That dog continued digging. He stopped, puzzled, when the carpet came up between his paws and he was face-to-face with blank wood instead of rats.

"Need some help?" My voice quavered.

That dog ignored me. He just stared down at the floor like he couldn't figure out why he wasn't chasing rats right that second.

"You stupid dog." I sighed. I stepped from couch to coffee table and jumped onto the old brown chair. I leaned over and picked him up. He turned his head a little and growled at me.

He weighed maybe all of ten pounds. His wiry fur crackled unpleasantly between my fingers and

I could feel his breath—wet, rotten doggy vapor—on the backs of my hands. His feet splayed in the air as I climbed with him over various pieces of furniture, into my bedroom and onto my bed, where I shoved him out the window.

"Go get 'em," I said.

After fifteen seconds of silence, the worst squealing I have ever heard broke out beneath the floor. A small, furry thud landed in the leaves outside. I hotfooted it back over the furniture onto the couch and clapped my hands over my ears. I hummed "Nearer My God to Thee" to drown out the snarls and squeaks echoing under the floor.

When I reached the third verse, it was quiet.

I peeled my hands off my ears and listened nervously. It stayed quiet. Eventually, I stood up and peeked out a window. Leaves had been kicked up everywhere. Mom's lawn chair was knocked over. The cover on the gas grill was crooked.

Slowly I opened the kitchen door. The rat-catcher was trotting briskly across our concrete patio, a squirmy brown body clamped delicately between his canine teeth. At the edge of the windbreak, that dog stopped and looked over his shoulder at me. The rat, four bitty paws and a hairless tail churning mightily for escape, gave a sharp squeal.

I slammed the door, raced to my room, and slammed that door, too. I hid under the blankets and moaned faintly into my pillow. Pretty soon I heard the thump of that dog jumping through my window. I froze in terror. He nosed around my room. Then he sniffed the line of air under my door like he was rat-checking the rest of the house.

Not a growl, not a whine. That dog remained blessedly silent. I lifted my head. The house remained blessedly silent.

He glanced up at me and snarled. Then he curled up in the box of dirty laundry in my closet and went to sleep. I lay there on my bed and slowly unfroze. I was exhausted. That dog started to snore.

Just before I drifted off to sleep, I glanced at the clock. Seven twenty-two A.M. That dog had cleared out our rat population in twenty-two minutes flat. Glory Hallelujah.

Chapter Six

That was about it for the rats.

When I woke up, it was noon and the dog was gone. I lay in bed like always, and spent a few minutes drawing a line down the middle of *Saturday*. Naturally, I started with

Chores

1. Get up.
2. Clean bedroom. Wash sheets.
3. Vacuum living room. Tack down the carpet behind the chair before Mom sees it.
4. Keep quiet about the ratcatcher.

(A) The trailer park charges extra rent for dogs.
(B) Especially ugly, bad-tempered killer dogs.

5. Homework: Start and finish today.

I thought about moving number 5 higher up the list. After all, Sunday would be a wasted day as far as homework went. MaryEllen's mom and dad were going to Columbus for a Republican fund-raiser, and MaryEllen had asked me along to spend the day with her at the zoo.

The second column remained a blank white space. I listened hard for any rat scrabble coming from the crawl space. Nothing. At least nothing I could hear over the sound of Mom banging away, cleaning up the kitchen.

Hmmm. I tried hard to think of something easy and safe to fill up that empty half of the page in my head. Trouble was, everything I ever had to do in my life, I had already done. I had nothing left over for a dull *Saturday*. Nothing, that is, except

The Truth

1. Drag myself out of bed.
2. Drag myself down the hall. Into the kitchen.
3. Nail Mom to the wall with my stunning grasp of the truth.

I pulled the covers over my head. Too bad I didn't have a big pink eraser handy.

Fifteen minutes later I gave up. Slowly, I dragged myself out of bed. Slowly, slowly I dragged myself down the hall. I had had a series of midnight frights, a brisk morning bike ride, and then, on about four hours of sleep I had *The Truth*. I was beat. I had a headache. Everything looked wavy and bleached out, like I was living under water.

I waded ashore into the kitchen and promptly

slashed my big toe open on a glass shard from a broken pickle jar. While I was hopping around bleeding, the phone rang. Doc Henderson wanted to know if I'd bring him another *New York Times* from the Duke. Mom handed me a paper towel and decided since she had the stove pulled out, she might as well clean the wall behind it and fix the busted burner. She got out the steel wool and her pliers and started to whistle.

I hung up the phone and dabbed at my bloody toe. *Face it*, I told myself sternly. *Face her*. But my mind went totally blank.

That's when MaryEllen banged on the door.

"Hi, Larch! Hi, Mrs. Waysorta!"

MaryEllen coaxed me outside to "sit on the steps, inn't a nice day, did you just get up, tell me you haven't been wearing those jeans since Friday, what's with your toe?" MaryEllen was talking way too much, even for MaryEllen. She was up to something.

Of course, I checked out the windbreak first

thing, ready to be grossed out. No rats. No rat-catcher. What a relief.

And it was a nice day, the sky a big bowl of blue shaking down over the chocolate dirt. The air was so clear, it hurt my tired lungs to breathe it. I straightened the cover on the grill and sat down in Mom's lawn chair. I waited for MaryEllen to plunk down on the top step like she usually did. Instead, she stood way clear of the steps, stood in the overgrown windbreak between the school field and our trailer, really, and kind of stuck out her chest.

"What in the world are you doing?" I asked.

"Um. You know. Sitting, talking, you know."

"MaryEllen, you are certainly not sitting, and as for talking, you—"

Noise from the schoolyard drifted across the open field.

"Hmmm," I said. "Tom Prouty's playing basketball at the school."

"Is he looking over here?" asked MaryEllen eagerly.

"Who can tell? He's all the way over by the basketball hoop. He is so far away, I'd never know it was him except one of those itty-bitty figures has just skinnied up a pole, and now he's pretending to pick big old boogers out of his nose and wipe them on the backboard, so I *know* it's gotta be—"

MaryEllen step-hopped into the school field. "Like, is he looking this way now?"

I was disgusted. "He's too busy with his nose, MaryEllen. Give it a rest."

But she didn't. So we stayed like that for about twenty minutes, shooting conversation at each other across fifteen feet of trees and bushes until the boys left the schoolyard.

After that MaryEllen dragged me all over Pottsville, walking and talking out her crazy mixed-up feelings for Tom Prouty. But hey, I had a few mixed-up feelings, too. And there was my best friend. Somebody I could talk to. You know, say anything to.

So I told her about the lost *New York Times*. I told her I cut my toe on a broken pickle jar. I told her I had homework.

"Yeah, me too," she said as we went inside the Duke. "But we can do it in the car coming home from the zoo tomorrow."

We talked to Mr. King at the Duke. We walked the paper clear across town to the Hendersons' and visited with them under the skylights for a while. We left and wandered around for another hour. We bumped into Shannon Brewster and Mindy Hardcastle from MaryEllen's Learning Team at school. We talked and talked.

Finally, I told MaryEllen I was dead tired. I told her my toe was killing me. I told her it was suppertime. I told her I was going home.

I limped home. I hung up my jacket and patted

the carpet back into place with my uninjured foot. Mom said we were out of hot dogs, were TV dinners okay? I said sure. I said we had the cleanest stove on the planet. I said I had a bunch of homework.

So. Saturday evening, I faced it. I was hopeless. I had talked to everybody about everything today, hoping to limber up, but I couldn't start a conversation about my father's murder.

That evening, Mom sat on the couch and smoked and watched TV. I sat in the brown chair across the room with my homework on my lap and studied her gorgeous face. She sat so silent, still as stone, like I wasn't in the same room with her. Like I had never been in the same room with her. And every time I thought I might speak up—one, two, eight times—honestly, my brain went numb. My heart froze. So weird. I couldn't figure it out.

I blinked at my algebra assignment where the

x's yielded nothing but *y*'s. For the first time ever, I was stuck. On algebra. On my stupid life.

Mom went to bed. I went to bed. The house was silent. As I lay there in the dark trying to get some sleep, the ratcatcher jumped through my window and bounced onto the bed. His furry body brushed my cheek.

Hmmm. What was that smell? That was not the smell of a sweet little doggie that had spent a sunny fall day innocently chasing rabbits. It was the smell of a vicious mutt that had spent the day snapping at rat tails and eating old people's garbage. And it was surely not a smell I wanted lolling around on my bedspread.

I gave the ratcatcher a poke with my foot. "Okay, pal, off the bed," I said. That dog growled at me.

I got up and opened the window a little wider. I thought about spending the night on the couch, but Mom might come out and ask me what was up so I suffered in silence, shivering on the floor, wrapped in the one measly blanket the ratcatcher agreed to let me have, until Mom left for work at three A.M.

Mom firmly believes that one day our trailer will burst into flames between the time she goes to work and the time I get up for my paper route. So every morning before she leaves, she turns off all the power to our trailer—electricity, heat, everything. Then she tests all the battery-powered smoke detectors, carbon monoxide monitors, and door alarms she's installed over the years. So I am used to being jolted from sleep at three A.M. by *beeep-beeeep, screeech, waaaah, ding-ding-ding, ahwoooo, 'bye, honey, stay under those covers!*

"'Bye, honey," she called. "Stay under those covers!"

Instead of rolling over and going back to sleep, I got up and turned the power back on. Yawning, I slouched into the bathroom.

I didn't know much about dog hygiene and didn't really care, but I had seen all those movies where The Little Kid Gives the Big Dog a Bath. The bathroom gets trashed of course; mountains of soap bubbles, water all over the floor; the dog does the big shakeroo. The kid scrubs the dog's teeth with the mom's toothbrush. Yuk, yuk, yuk.

I filled the tub with three inches of warm water. I put plastic sheeting on the floor. I got out my own shampoo. I got out every single towel we owned. I put on an old yellow raincoat from the closet. And I got out a package of fish sticks from the freezer.

"Here, doggie, doggie," I called.

The ratcatcher came. He stood in the doorway, blinking and watchful, as I waggled a fish stick in his direction. Suddenly he lowered his blunt head to the floor and whined.

I froze. My hand clenched around the fish stick as the ratcatcher prowled through the house, growling at the fresh rat scent under the trailer. The crawl space echoed with nervous rat squeaks. That dog growled louder. The trailer walls vibrated faintly as another army of rats fled through cracks and holes and scurried away into the dark. After a few minutes the ratcatcher, blessedly silent, appeared in the bathroom doorway.

I might have crouched there a good long while by the bathtub, heart thumping, smashed fish stick in my hand, had not that dog simply stepped into the bathtub. Unbelievable. I dropped the fish stick in surprise. That dog chased it through the water and ate it.

I cupped a handful of warm water and poured it carefully over his shoulders. The ratcatcher wagged his tail briefly and licked at my fishy hand.

"You like getting wet?" I asked in astonishment.

Apparently he did. That dog closed his eyes in pleasure and grunted. I wetted him down and squirted on shampoo. Gently, in case he was getting ready to open his mouth and snap, I soaped his barrel chest and short, bowed legs. He sighed happily. I soaped over the spine bones bumping under his skin and squeezed out the foam along his bony tail. That dog was nothing more than muscle and sinew wrapped in a thin layer of coarse hair and dog skin.

Awful dog. Of course, I was totally grateful to the ratcatcher for scaring away the rats. I'd become his devoted slave of the bath, hadn't I? Fed him hot dogs and let him hog the bed, hadn't I? But I loathed him, his spirit. Awful, nasty, killer dog.

My heart was hard, but I did my duty. I soaped him up good two times, added a little more hot water, and rubbed in conditioner. I thought it might make his fur feel soft like fur instead of like a used pot scrubber.

I ran the blow-dryer over him while he snacked on a couple of fish sticks. I turned off the dryer and took a cautious sniff. Hmmm. Now he smelled like rat tails, old people's garbage, and coconut shampoo. His hair was the same scraggy, dingy white. Nothing had changed. He was still the same ugly, liver-spotted ratcatcher that had followed my hot dogs home.

I cleared my throat and reached out to pat him. "Um. Good dog," I said.

That dog ignored me. He leaned over and nosed the last fish stick out of the package. Wearily, I nudged him aside and straightened up what little mess there was. Mom slopped more water on the floor than this mutt did. When I left for my paper route, he was curled up asleep on my bed.

I dragged myself over my paper route, came home, pushed the dog off my bed, and fell across it. He jumped beside me and snarled in my ear until I stumbled to the kitchen and microwaved him a burrito. I fell back into bed.

Five minutes later the alarm went off. Sunday morning, eight A.M. I opened my eyes and moaned. I had half an hour before the Stillwaters picked me up for a fun-filled day at the zoo.

Chapter Seven

I started flunking school.

What next?

The next Friday afternoon when the dismissal bell rang, Mrs. Marilyn said, "Larch? Stay behind. Please."

Her tone was a cross between nice Mrs. Marilyn and crabby Mrs. Hogstettler. I dragged myself over to her desk by the windows. MaryEllen, the last one to leave, threw me a mournful look.

"Larch. I don't need to tell you how poor your school performance has been this week," began Marilyn Hogstettler.

I rubbed my red-rimmed eyes. Teachers always *say* they don't have to tell you how you goofed up, and then they go over all the stupid details anyway.

"On Monday you hadn't completed any of the weekend homework. Tuesday, you flunked the history test—"

"D-plus," I interrupted. "I got a D-plus."

"Excuse me. A D-plus," said Mrs. Hogstettler. "A D-plus preceded by a row of A's as long as your arm in my grade book. I talked to you on Tuesday, too. Do you remember?"

Of course I remembered. I remembered mumbling a whole string of *yes ma'ams* and *no ma'ams* while looking down at my history test and this big, fat, red D (plus). The Hog made her D's spiky and outsized, more like coat hangers than D's. I remembered thinking: *My first D. At least it's a D-plus.*

"Wednesday, you failed to have a single snapshot ready for the photo montage. Thursday, you mumbled something about needing a little more time for the written part of your *Who's Who* project." Mrs. Hog's eyes narrowed. "Out of the kindness of my heart, Larch, I gave you an extension."

I had to yawn.

"But we agreed, Larch, that you would hand in your completed project first thing Friday morning. *This* morning."

I had to yawn. I would not yawn. I had to yawn. My eyes watered with the effort not to yawn.

"So. Where was it?"

Frankly, I had been so wrapped up in not yawning, I had forgotten that the final, ultimate, take-no-prisoners deadline for my *Who's Who* on Mr. Prouty had been that morning.

I yawned.

"All week," said the Hog, "the Boosters have been setting up for Founder's Day tomorrow. They convinced First Baptist's Board of Elders to loan out the church's one-hundred-fifty-two-year-old hand-carved oak lectern to display our class project. That historic lectern with our book on it is supposed to sit on the right hand of the Veterans of Foreign Wars memorabilia display and on the left hand of a diorama depicting the life and accomplishments of Edward Potts. That's how highly the Boosters put this project."

The Hog glanced at the clock. "In ten minutes, Larch, a Booster will come for this great work of our hands and our hearts—*Who's Who of Pottsville, Ohio*. This means I have about nine minutes to figure out how to explain that *Who's Who* profiles everybody except Charles Randall Prouty. Beloved school custodian. Father of seven. Swan County's most decorated Vietnam War veteran. And a direct descendant of Jonathan Prouty, who cleared Potts's trace through the Ohio wilderness side by side with Edward Potts himself. 'Sorry,' I'll say. 'One of our students forgot. Maybe we should just move the lectern next to the pickle-judging contest.'"

Angrily, the Hog plugged one nostril and took a few deep cleansing breaths. Slowly, Mrs. Marilyn got a grip and tried a different approach.

"Have you started your period, Larch dear?"

"Jeez, Mrs. Marilyn!"

"Well then, what is it?"

A good question. I stared out the windows at the empty playground. The weather had turned sunless and damp. Since the rats were cleaned out, hordes of mice were making a run for the cracks and crevices into our house trailer. The busy ratcatcher, jumping silently through my window, started most of his shrieking mousie battles after Mom went to work. Sleepless and tense every night, waiting for combat to begin, I was getting zero sleep.

Forget sleep. Waking was a nightmare, too. That morning, for instance, I had wandered drowsily into the bathroom, where I just about stepped on a little gray mouse busy digging through the overturned wastebasket. My steam-whistle shrieks must have scared it silly, because that mouse jumped straight up and keeled over in a dead faint right in front of the toilet.

I ran into my room. "Get up, you stupid dog!" I screeched. "There's an unconscious mouse in the bathroom! Do something!" I pushed him off the bedspread. He just growled at me, climbed into the box of dirty laundry in my closet, and shut his eyes.

I had to get out the broom and sweep that groggy mouse through the hallway, into the kitchen, and out the door. All by myself. In my *underwear.*

Then there was the little matter of asking happy, perky, nicey questions to the guy who laid on me the news that my mother had killed my father—accidently. Right, sure, sure. The guy who told me the truth. Maybe that was Mr. Prouty's guiding principle in life, telling the truth. A principle my mother sure wasn't aware of. She skittered around the truth every time: worked nights, slept a lot, skipped church, avoided her kid—drifting in her deep, dark, safe, and quiet night.

For the thousandth-and-twelfth time since last Friday, my mind went round and round. Thousandth-and-twelfth, same as the first. A little bit louder and a little bit worse.

Mrs. Marilyn was waiting for me to say something. I couldn't remember what we had been talking about. I tried not to yawn.

"Um," I said.

She looked at me a long, long time. Finally, she eased the schoolbooks out of my hands. "You're excused from homework this weekend, Larch. Go home. Take a nap. Have a little fun at Founder's Day tomorrow. When you want to talk, I want to listen."

She patted my hand. "Next week will be better, dear. I know it will be. Otherwise"—the Hog flashed across Mrs. Marilyn's sympathetic expression—"I'll call your mother."

I staggered across the school field, focused on Mrs. Marilyn's wonderful nap suggestion. The wind was breaking up the afternoon clouds. Here and there shafts of sunlight lit up the field. The wet grass gleamed brown and gold and orange. Purple asters and goldenrod shook beads of water from their heads, windblown, now in sunlight, now in shadow. And in the middle of this warm and mellow autumn scene, doddery old Mr. Wilkins from three trailers over was poking the tip of his cane through the dead twig underbrush beneath my bedroom window.

"Hey, Mr. Wilkins," I said, all warm and mellow.

"Fluffy didn't come home last night," he said in his quavery voice. "I called for her and called for her."

"Fluffy? Your old cat?" I said, a horrible thought slowly forming in the back of my brain.

"Fluffy always comes home when I call for her." Mr. Wilkins's cheeks were red and chapped.

He'd been out here a long time already, tottering around the trailer park, sweet-talking his cat. Here, kitty. Here kitty, kitty.

"I don't know what to think," he said fretfully. He stirred his cane through the wet leaves at the edge of our patio. "I don't know what to think."

Boy. I knew what to think. My fingers clutched at my stone-cold stomach. I knew exactly what to think. The ratcatcher couldn't be bothered to chase one puny little mouse out of the bathroom, because he had moved on to bigger and better prey. Like harmless old Mr. Wilkins's cat.

Slowly my hands moved away from my stomach and clutched at my heart. Which felt like it was going to fly right out between my ribs.

I hated the ratcatcher. I loathed that dog—

—"like Mom," I muttered out loud. Finally. "Like I hate you, Mom."

Wait a minute. I lived by

Even More Rules

1. Honor your mother.
2. Ace out school.
3. Be kind to small dogs and children.

What a bunch of stupid, stupid rules.

Any minute now my head, filled with The Rules Are the Rules, would explode and burn down the whole trailer park. I was a red-hot stove going full blast, burning up with secrets and car crashes and silences and rats and D-pluses; cooking down to the bone—

Nope. No more.

Mr. Wilkins faded away behind the Boulsons' trailer, calling for Fluffy. Me, I got out the hammer and nailed my bedroom window shut. The rats were welcome to the crawl space. Mice could live in our bathroom. I would keep my toothbrush at the Duke and comb my hair at school.

But if that dog came around here one more time, I'd borrow Tom Prouty's hunting rifle and take aim and blow him headless. Mom wouldn't care.

Chapter Eight

The wind blew away all the clouds during the night in which I slept and slept and then overslept. It was like the old days before I knew about the rats under the trailer. Days of dutiful ignorance about the truth, and seriousness about the rules; nights of blank, dreamless sleep.

So. I woke up to brilliant blue skies and wind whistling through the branches, shaking down the brown leaves of Pottsville's hundred-year-old oaks. The last leaves of the season. The minute I left the house, late for the ten-o'clock parade, I knew. That day was not just Founder's Day. It was the last, great day of fall.

Down the sidewalk, running. Twelve hours of sleep, no homework all weekend, and a sunlit, quiet bathroom free from rodent ambush had made me light-headed and happy. Like it'd be possible to get my life under control. Put everything back where it belonged.

Running, running, running. I raised my arms to fly. Ohioans have a proud history of flight. The Wright brothers. Neil Armstrong. Judith Resnik. John Glenn—twice now, as a matter of fact. I had just one list for that day. So pure and simple I called it

The Founder's Day Rules

1. Do not ask Elaine Mae Waysorta (mother) a direct question about her husband, Christopher Allen Waysorta (deceased).
2. Do not ask Larch Anne Waysorta (daughter) to discuss her feelings

about the father (deceased), as named above.

3. Do not leave dirty underwear on the bathroom floor.

That list sounded great to me. The rules are the rules are the rules. After all, those three simple rules had made me what I was: a good girl, a moral girl; excellent academic record; no drugs or weird boyfriends—a girl making something out of her life. A girl whose parents would be proud, if one weren't dead and the other comatose.

It was okay. Mom took okay care of me. A little heavy on the junk food, maybe, but I could live with that. It was okay. I would be moderately grief-stricken, flying back to Pottsville for the funeral after she died of lung cancer. But that was okay too. It wouldn't be so hard. Did TV Lauren ever bother about her childhood? No way.

Truth was, it would be seven years, about. Seven more years and I would be eighteen years old. I'd be gone. I turned the corner and confidently strolled down Main Street. There was nothing and nobody to hold me. Until then I'd pay close attention to the rules, live by them faithfully. Eventually, the rules would set me free.

And wouldn't Founder's Day be a pleasant memory? Main Street, blocked off with sawhorses on either end, was packed with folks from all over the county. In a vacant lot turned car park, I spotted a couple of cars all the way from West Virginia. The Pottsville Boosters had gone all out and strung yellow and white balloons, club colors, between the streetlights. The happy squeaks of balloons rubbing in the wind and an occasional *pop!* colored every conversation, every speech, every pickle-judging contest of Founder's Day.

Five minutes after the end of the parade—which featured the mayor and his family in pioneer clothes waving from the back of a Cadillac convertible, a whole slew of Boosters dressed like Edward Potts and buckskinners and coal miners and Civil War widows, and the Pottsville Grammar Drum and Bugle Corps bringing up the rear—half the crowd whipped out card tables and boxes of junk from the trunks of their cars. Before the last bugle had finished blatting under the canopy of trees, a rip-roaring flea market marched right down the middle of Main Street.

The Duke of Donuts had set up a doughnut-and-cider wagon in front of the bank. Respectfully, dutifully, I helped Mom make change for a while. MaryEllen came by and bought a doughnut.

"Did you see me wave at you?" she asked.

"Uh-huh," I said. "Where'd you get the prairie dress?"

"Ugly, inn't it?" said MaryEllen. "Laura Ingalls Wilder meets Heidi in a dark alley. Mom, who has never voluntarily thrown anything out, wore this to her eighth-grade dance." She licked the glaze on her fingers. "I got to go home and change. Will your mom let you go? We could walk around and stuff. I said I'd sit for Ben Bentton at five, because his folks want to go to the square dance tonight."

So. We walked around for a while. The Boosters bought Mrs. Marilyn's explanation, whatever it was. *Who's Who of Pottsville, Ohio* sat on First Baptist's historic lectern right between the Edward Potts diorama and the veterans' display. Catty-corner was the Home Ec class's gingerbread railroad depot/dog pound.

"Lookit," said MaryEllen. "They used black frosting for water damage on the roof, and boarded up the broken window with a graham cracker. Cute, huh?"

As the last great morning of fall turned into the last great afternoon, MaryEllen and I ran into Tom Prouty in the secondhand bookstall. Literally. In the narrow aisle between two jammed tables, my elbow bumped a box of Harlequin romances and sent the box straight down on Tom's foot. Books flew everywhere.

"Ow, Larch!"

"Hey, Tom. Watch where you're standing."

But I said it kindly. I was mellow from twelve hours of sleep, no homework, and a whole afternoon of living by the rules.

Surprise, surprise. Instead of picking a fight Tom helped me dump the books back into the box. Then he shoved a paperback book in my face. His thumb went up my nose, practically.

"You ever read this?" he asked.

"*Riders of the Purple Sage*. Nope. You like Westerns, huh?"

"I think," said Tom Prouty fervently, "that Zane Grey was the greatest writer who ever lived."

I stared at Tom Prouty, student goof-off. Based on his performance at school, I was amazed he knew *how* to read. Then he started waving his arms and yelling that western adventure was the most underrated genre of them all.

Genre? Huh?

MaryEllen, who was at the other end of the bookstall sorting through the largest collection of old *People* magazines on the planet, looked up at the noise and made a beeline over to Tom Prouty's side.

She glanced at the title and said, "I read that."

Tom stopped in midwave. "What?" he asked.

"Um," said MaryEllen. "Last summer. The library has a bunch of Zane Grey's books and I—"

"You," said Tom excitedly. "You're the one. I noticed the date due stamp on the inside covers. A different book went out every week. Man! I wanted to meet you! Someone who appreciates Grey's genius—"

"Um . . ."

"His style—"

"Well . . ."

"His manly men—"

"Hold it!" exclaimed MaryEllen.

I gaped at these two people that I had gone to school with since kindergarten. I thought I knew them. But gorgeous Tom Prouty looked like he had just won a million bucks because he had discovered who checked out a bunch of moldy old books from the library's fiction section. And sweet, kind MaryEllen was getting . . . mad.

"I *enjoyed* Grey's books, Tom. I *liked* them. But to say that Zane Grey is a genius is way too much."

Tom drew back. "Oh? Name one writer of Westerns that attains Grey's stature."

MaryEllen shrugged. Casually. "Terry C. Johnston."

"That fraud!"

MaryEllen shrugged again. "Louis L'Amour."

"Grey invented the Western!"

She scratched her nose. "Adele C. Brighton."

"A woman!"

MaryEllen pounced. "Aha! I knew it! Scared to read from a woman's point of view!"

Tom jumped up and down, fizzing and popping. I elbowed MaryEllen in the ribs. "How come you know so much about books, MaryEllen?" I asked.

"Well. I do a lot of baby-sitting. There's never anything good on TV."

I was about to ask her if she had seen *Fitz*'s big smooch-with-Lauren's-neighbor-in-the-bathroom scene when she glanced at her watch. "Oops. Gotta go."

"Wait a minute," said Tom. "We're not done here. I'm coming with you."

MaryEllen smiled radiantly. Tom stopped and really looked at her for the first time since first grade. I swear, MaryEllen looked . . . drop-dead gorgeous. Tom blinked. Off they walked, discussing Zane Grey and his genre. His genius. Whatever.

What next?

I tried to remember the last book I read not for school, but for myself. Hmmm. And the way those two had bent red-faced over the book in Tom's hand, balloons squeaking over their heads, yelling at each other. They'd been having a great time.

I had nothing like that. Oh, I had the smart-as-a-whip, grade-skipper thing. I had the blank-sheet-of-paper, list-of-things-to-do thing. I frowned. And for a split second I had this vision of Mom and her cigarette stuck outside a big, empty space where past the dark is my dad, it really is my dad, only this time she's not pushing me back, she's grabbing my arm, grabbing both arms, whispering hang on, Larch, you and me will go in together.

So weird. I got a big cloud of her ciggie smoke straight in my face. It made me cough. I had to blink away the stinging tears. Right there on Main Street. My heart started to pound. I didn't know why.

Okay, maybe I was crazy mixed-up on the inside, feeling her arms slide around me like that. But on the outside, I acted like I always do. Nice girl; good girl; smart girl. I wandered back to the doughnut wagon, dutifully helped Mom and Dora pack up. They waved good-bye and drove back to the Duke. I walked home.

The sun had almost set. The wind whisked oak leaves around my ankles. I walked around the crackly drifts of leaves and kept to the barren, windswept sidewalk. I stuffed my hands in my pockets and walked slow; slower. Part of me tried, tried, tried to get those phantom arms to hold me again. The other part concentrated on moving along.

That was when I heard the yelling in the Benttons' backyard.

I couldn't think what in the world MaryEllen was doing in the Benttons' backyard until I remembered she was baby-sitting Ben while his parents went to the Founder's Day square dance. She was huddled on the top step of the porch, Ben clamped between her knees. Her screams went off right in the poor little kid's ear, which was why Ben was pounding on her legs and shrieking at the top of his three-year-old lungs "*LegGOaME!*" Both of them were covered with grass and dirt.

I grabbed MaryEllen's shoulder and shook her screamless. "What is your problem, MaryEllen?" I demanded. Ben hiccupped. For a second, it was totally quiet.

Except for a lot of growling.

I saw Ben's little red wagon. I saw his stuffed animals bleeding their fluffy white guts out all over the backyard. And I saw the ratcatcher crouched in the wagon bed. He dug and shook and ripped into the few pathetic toys still in the wagon. Polyester fiberfill snowed down around his head.

"Ben was marching around, playing F-F-Founder's Day PArade with his wagon full of stuffed animals," whimpered MaryEllen, "and I was sitting HEre just about to call him in when that DOG RAn out of the woods grOWLing. Ben WEnt to run and TRipped over the wagon handle and I swear, L-L-Larch, that's all that saved him from a deaTH Bite. That dog hit the wagON so hard, the wagon coaSTed backward about three F-F-Feet, and iT's been tearing out the hearts OF All Ben's little stuffed kiTTies and buNNies . . ."

MaryEllen trailed off. Ben started to wail again.

My heart thundered, at one with the wind and the night and the screams and the panicky fear. I knew that dog. I knew him. I backed up the stairs, fell through the screen door into the Benttons' kitchen, picked up the phone, and in a stuttering voice, told the operator to connect me with AnIMAl WelfaRE, pu-puh, puh-lease.

Chapter Nine

Two guys in a bright blue dog pound van pulled up about five minutes after the ratcatcher left off the attack and trotted silently into the woods. They found us three humans still glued to the porch.

MaryEllen was amazing. She told the whole story pretty calmly to the guy in charge, then pointed off to the woods.

"He went thataway," said MaryEllen Zane Grey.

By that time it was dark. The guy was holding a penlight to the notebook he had resting on his potbelly. He scribbled for a minute. "'Zat a dog you recognize?"

"No way," said MaryEllen.

"Bad dog," said Ben.

Hmmm. Here was my big opportunity to admit I had fed and sheltered a mad dog. A potential child killer. *Yessir, I know it's hard to believe, sir, but that ugly killer dog has been hogging my bed this last week.*

As MaryEllen had said, no way. No way was I going to admit breaking the rules. Breaking Pottsville's leash laws by encouraging a killer dog to roam loose around the neighborhood. Breaking the trailer park's pet rent rule by letting that dog jump in and out my bedroom window for free. Hey, I wasn't even going to admit stealing all those hot dogs out of my own refrigerator.

So I kept quiet. MaryEllen kept talking. The guy with the penlight kept scribbling. Pretty soon it was like MaryEllen was talking for both of us. Like I was the shy one. Like maybe I didn't have anything to do with it at all.

The guy flipped his notebook closed. His

partner pulled a wire choke noose attached to a long metal pole out of the back of the van. He stuck a package of hot dogs into his coat pocket.

The dogcatchers walked into the woods. Mary-Ellen and Ben went inside to call the Benttons at the square dance. I stayed outside.

Boy. I was sick to death of that horrible dog. Dead rats, fainting mice, missing cats, mangled stuffed animals. Once those guys lured the rat-catcher's neck into the noose with a couple of hot dogs—easy enough thanks to me; that dog trusted a human hand holding out a hot dog—they'd take him to the pound and gas him after twenty-four hours as a dangerous animal. More killing, but I'd never lay eyes on that dog again.

All I had to do was keep on doing what I was already doing. Not say a square word. That dog would be gone. Not a thing in this world would remind me of him. Eventually, everything would settle to the bottom of my brain. The ratcatcher would become a memory buried under eighth-grade science and the high school prom and my first hot tub with a skylight. I'd never think about him again. My hands rubbed my face, once, twice. So weird. It was Mom's closed, silent face under my fingertips. I didn't know why.

Mr. and Mrs. Bentton came home in a screech of tires and loud, worried voices. They went inside and fussed over Ben. MaryEllen came out with two flashlights and a garbage bag, and we started to clean up the mess in the backyard. That's when we made an important discovery.

"Yuck," said MaryEllen.

The polyester fluff all around the wagon was covered with gore. With the head of my flashlight, I eased aside a blood-soaked giraffe. A snake—very long, very black, and totally dead—lay kinked across the blue plush back of a smiling kangaroo.

MaryEllen swallowed hard. "You don't suppose . . ."

That horrible dog

". . . he killed that snake . . ."

to protect Ben?

". . . to save Ben?" said MaryEllen. "And we called the dog pound?"

"You've read too many hero dog books," I said shortly. I stared at the broken snake. *Not a scratch, not a bruise* nagged unpleasantly in my mind.

"Well, I sure don't think this snake crawled in the wagon to die of old age," said MaryEllen indignantly. "That dog is innocent."

"Not totally innocent," I muttered, remembering Mr. Wilkins's missing cat, Fluffy. "But I know what you mean."

And I did, too. Maybe if I had said something about that dog's dirty little war on rodents, the animal welfare guys might have looked around. They'd have found the dead snake; they'd have tossed the choke noose into the van and fed the ratcatcher a whole lot of hot dogs. *Good boy. Good doggie.*

But I'd said squat. My silence had set them loose. A couple of regular guys out doing their job, collecting and destroying a dangerous animal.

But really I had—just hesitated a little. Paused to collect my thoughts. That's all it was. Nothing bad. Right?

I turned back to the wagon. The wind clashed through the tree branches. I might have stayed like that until morning, staring at a dead snake, surrounded by my guilt and the night wind, had not those fateful words popped out of my mouth:

"Boy, MaryEllen. What next?"

"We go to the pound," said MaryEllen positively, "and see."

I shut off my flashlight. The click sounded like gritted teeth. The last thing I wanted to do was see that ugly dog again. I wanted to crawl in bed, pull the covers over my head, and let the years roll by this whole nasty thing.

"MaryEllen, leave it. I'm tired," I said.

"We can't leave it!" she cried. "That dog is

going to die because of us! We gotta do something!"

MaryEllen is my best friend. We have played together since we were babies, and frankly, good old MaryEllen is a pushover. But the MaryEllen who grabbed my arm in the Benttons' backyard that night and dragged me across town to the dog pound was no kind of pushover. Okay, so MaryEllen had always been a friend to the animals and stuff. But where did she get such a red-hot sense of injustice?

Well. The dog pound—Pottsville's historic train depot—sits next to a pair of abandoned railroad tracks not far from the river. By the time we got there it was eight o'clock and the employees were long gone. But the blue van was parked near the front entrance under a light shining on the gravel driveway.

MaryEllen rattled the double doors. "Locked," she said.

I leaned one shoulder against the wall and started thinking.

Not like I wanted to help that stupid dog, but I did want to know if he was actually in the dog pound. No way did I want him rattling my window tonight. I figured if he was safely locked up, we could call the next morning and tell them about the snake. Wait a minute. The next day was Sunday. Okay, we'd call Monday after school. And a sad voice on the other end would tell us sorry, the poor little guy had been sent to doggie heaven.

Under the weak light the bricks gleamed faintly, like squares of moist, dark cake. It was why the eighth-grade Home Ec class wanted to bake a gingerbread depot instead of a white sheet cake with safe, dignified roses . . . complete with a broken window boarded up with a graham cracker. Hmmm.

"Come on," I said to MaryEllen, and disappeared around the corner.

The broken window was covered with cheap particle board. A couple of nails let go with my first experimental yank. I grinned at MaryEllen and yanked harder.

"Whoops," I said.

The board snapped in half. The broken piece flew out of my hands over our heads and landed in the bushes.

A big, black scary hole into the dog pound gaped about eye-level at us. The smell of wild and lonely animals in too small cages with too few cleanings drifted past our noses. There was a breath of silence. Then we heard a hundred toe-nails *click click click* on the tile floor as the dogs stopped dozing and climbed to their feet.

"Poor things," whispered MaryEllen.

She elbowed me aside and pulled herself through the window space. She landed with a muffled thump. Low growls rose from inside.

Cautiously, I dropped down next to her and switched on the Benttons' flashlight. My jaw dropped. We were standing in the back of a long, narrow room, the old depot's first-class passenger lounge. It was now the main dog kennel. My flashlight beam bounced from an elegant vine-and-leaf floor mosaic to a double row of rusty metal cages. Directly across from us was a solid oak door inlaid with leaded glass panes. I turned the tarnished brass door handle. A mop and bucket leaned against a rolltop desk as tall as my head.

In my mind, I heard the whisper of soft, laughing voices and the swish of silk skirts rustling over the blue and white floor tiles. In my mind, I saw women with beaded purses and swooping flowered hats; men who smelled of rich tobacco and wore watch chains heavy with gold fobs. I touched the rolltop's great, curving side. It was scarred and stained, streaked with grime; still, the oak grain was warm and alive under my fingers.

"This place is a wonder," I said.

MaryEllen ignored me. She was halfway down the first row of cages, shining her flashlight lovingly on each whining, slobbering animal. "You poor, poor thing," she crooned, "all caged up—*ooooooo*, Larch, lookit! A whole bunch of kitties!"

Most of the wall next to the double-door entrance had been meshed in and turned into a cat compound. Dozens of red-eyed cats glared at me. A huge orange cat crouched alone at the top of a homemade cat tree. She looked like she weighed thirty-five pounds and ate skinny pre-teenagers for a midnight snack. One chewed ear grazed the chicken wire strung over the top of the cage. Right above her head hung an oil-lamp chandelier that had been converted to electricity. It sported twelve bulbs and a hundred teardrop prisms, every one of which was furred over by decades of dust and cat hair.

"This place is a dump," I said. My attention snapped back to the ill-tempered orange cat high above my head. I frowned. "Wait a minute. Don't I know that cat?"

"Sure you do. That's Mr. Wilkins's Fluffy," said MaryEllen as she shined her flashlight full in the cat's hairy face. Fluffy squinted and hissed. "Now how do you suppose she ended up here? Fluffy always goes home when Mr. Wilkins calls for her."

The ratcatcher hadn't killed Fluffy. The ratcatcher hadn't attacked Ben Bentton. Suddenly, I had a perfect memory of that dog trotting briskly across our patio, a rat dangling from his jaws. Hmmm. The rat hadn't been squeaking in fear, exactly. More like—annoyance. Since the ratcatcher had been hanging around my hot dogs, as far as I knew, he hadn't hurt a single rat. Fact was, that dog was the pure opposite of a dangerous animal. He had protected Ben. He was a hero.

I closed my eyes, totally sick and sorry. Everything I believed about that dog was a lie. And everything I'd done to him was plain wrong. It was me. I was the dangerous one here.

A low, mangy, rat-tailed whine made me open my eyes. The ratcatcher was stretched out alone in a small cage near the entrance. When I crouched down next to him, my shoulder brushed against a metal sign wired to the bars. TWENTY-FOUR HOUR HOLD ONLY.

What next?

The ratcatcher growled at me. He stopped in midgrowl and licked carefully, like it hurt to swallow, like it had been a bad business with the choke noose. Boy, I hated myself. I hated him. Even steven. I looked at that stupid, ugly, misbegotten dog and I said,

"So. Why are you here, really? Because I didn't tell the truth? Because it's the way things go? You're brave, you know that? The ugliest, bravest hero dog on the planet, locked up in this wonderful dump and tomorrow, pal, somebody's gonna kill you. All because of a misunderstanding."

A misunderstanding I had encouraged with plenty of hot dogs and warm snoozes on my bedspread and a cold fear of rodents. I leaned against the wire mesh and rubbed my aching head.

"A misunderstanding. Who am I trying to kid?" I murmured.

I hadn't exactly been chasing after the truth here. I had been so busy nailing shut my own hard-hearted judgments—that dog was a rat killer, my mother was a murderer, our school was a dump, and I was the poor, innocent victim—that I saw only what I wanted to see. That I believed only what I wanted to believe. I stared at that dog stretched out like death in his cage.

Like Mom. Exactly like Mom and all her years of silence. The ratcatcher whined softly while my mind got it. Totally, absolutely got it.

"It's the whole truth, pal," I told him. "Not just the easy part that makes you feel righteous and smart and angry. You've got to consider the whole truth. Even the part that makes you sick and sorry." I sighed mightily. "*Especially* the part that makes you sick and sorry."

I fingered the dead bolt on his cage. "The whole truth," I murmured, "and nothing but the truth.

Because when you know the truth, the truth will set you—"

One second later I was watching my poor thumb bleed where I had smashed it as I shot the cage-door bolt open. Flung wide the metal door. And set that ratcatcher free.

Boy. That dog's throat was sore hurting, but there was not a thing wrong with his legs. He shot out past the cage door and leaped out the broken window like he'd been blown out of a cannon—not one glance backward, not one last farewell snarl for Larch Waysorta, Seeker of Truth. Rescuer of Hero Dogs.

"Yes!" bellowed MaryEllen in my ear. "That's right! Freedom! Ooooooo, run, boy, *run*!"

Overcome, I guess, by the glory of an ugly dog gaining his freedom, MaryEllen threw open another cage door. And another. And another, and another and—riot time. A big golden retriever ran over to the front doors and barked to be let out, so MaryEllen threw them open too.

Some dogs bolted out into the windswept night. Others milled around, barking and prancing and jumping on MaryEllen. One dog came over and stuck his slobby nose in my crotch.

"Get away from me, you stupid mutt," I yelped. He wagged his tail.

I myself opened a couple of cages before my natural feelings about dogs got the better of me. Pretty soon I calmed down and prodded three yappy little mutts toward the front door with my foot.

"Go on," I said. "Shoo. Ick."

MaryEllen was still sailing around the pound, crying "Liberation!" and "Freedom!" and stuff like that. She set her sights on the cat compound.

"MaryEllen! *Wait!*"

Too late. MaryEllen flipped open the door. Yowling and hissing, cats streaked for the front door. The dogs left off drooling over MaryEllen and let loose after the cats. A Great Dane knocked MaryEllen right off her feet.

"Hey!" she cried from the floor. "Bad dog!"

"Look, dog. Cats. Lots and lots of cats," I said to the slobby dog sniffing my kneecaps. "Guys like you chase cats. Go get 'em." I pushed him sideways toward the door.

Fluffy got so freaked, she leaped for the chandelier twelve feet above her head. She fell way short naturally, and landed on a pile of dog food sacks. Her back claws dug into the slippery paper and slashed through the topmost bag as she made another try for the light. That second time, Fluffy swung aboard the chandelier, but the bag slid off the pile and broke: a hundred pounds of dog kibble cascaded everywhere. The dog left off smelling me and ambled over to scarf up dog food. Thank goodness.

"Hey," said MaryEllen again. Suddenly she looked pale. Her hand slipped off the bolt on the last closed cage. The dog inside—part Labrador, part trombone—gave a frustrated howl.

The wind banged one of the front doors shut.

Aside from the dog eating kibble, the cat swinging from the chandelier, and the trombone yodeling in his cage, we were alone. All around us doors creaked back and forth as the wind curled through the empty cages. Fluffy meowed.

Faintly, above the Labrador's howling, we heard the wail of a siren. MaryEllen put both hands to her mouth.

"What have we done?" she whispered.

Me, I had just enough strength to open the door for the trombone. Why should he be the only one not to run free? He trotted out the front door and disappeared into the woods along the river just as a Pottsville patrol car pulled up and cut its siren and lights.

Chapter Ten

A huge shadow loomed through the open front door. Officer John Bainter is a big, big man. His thick fingers fumbled for the light switch by the door. When he found it, he used his thumb and forefinger in the most dainty way possible to flick on the lights.

Three of the twelve chandelier bulbs turned on. Fluffy shifted irritably at the yellow brightness under her paws. There we were—the cat, the dog eating kibble, MaryEllen, and me.

"What are you kids—" Officer Bainter took a step forward. Dog food crunched under his shoe.

I nodded at MaryEllen encouragingly. Any

minute she'd start talking, talking, talking, explaining a lot of—I looked around at the empty cages—stuff that needed explaining.

"Hmmm," said Officer Bainter. He looked at us more closely. "You, I know. MaryEllen Stillwater, right? Mayor Stillwater's kid?"

MaryEllen put her hands over her face and moaned.

"It was an accident," I blurted to Officer Bainter. "Would you believe?"

Apparently not. He hauled us down to the Pottsville Police Department and called our parents.

At the police station, MaryEllen and I sat side by side on orange plastic chairs in the holding room. The chairs had been bolted straight to the floor. Our chairs were right next to a door that opened into a long hallway. Officer Bainter used the phone at the booking desk across the hall.

A police officer walked down the hall and asked for the chief.

"He went home," said Officer Bainter, still on the phone.

A few minutes later the same police officer came back down the hall and said, "Jeez, he puked again." He opened the door to the room next to ours, rummaged around and reappeared, pushing a mop and bucket on wheels. I smelled raspberry-scented disinfectant.

I dug my elbow in MaryEllen's ribs. "Smell that. Smells just like school," I whispered to her.

MaryEllen ignored me. She didn't even turn her head at the sight of a fully armed police officer pushing a mop bucket. All she would say over and over was "My dad's gonna kill me."

"Yeah. Probably," I said.

"I mean, he's really, really gonna kill me."

"Poor MaryEllen."

"Remember when that *Great Sea Battles* special was on TV last spring and my brother, Eddie, dressed up like Winston Churchill and directed the evacuation of Dunkirk at the boat launch?

That cost the city five hundred dollars in bomb damage to the boat ramp. Dad yelled for a week.

"And remember about a year ago when somebody hot-wired the Route 22 stoplight so instead of red, yellow, and green it turned orange, purple, and brown, and the clinic got flooded with people who thought they'd gone color-blind?"

"Sure. I remember that."

"That was Eleanor."

"No kidding, your sister, Ellie, did that?"

MaryEllen nodded miserably. "That cost the city another five hundred. I thought Dad was going to explode. One of Dad's reelection promises was how he was going to crack down on lowlifes and their vandalism. He had this speech. 'Pottsville is a good town, full of good schools, good churches, and good morals. I pledge to keep it that way.'"

MaryEllen sighed heavily. "On the one hand, liberating the dog pound seems pretty tame after the Eddie and Ellie stuff. On the other hand"—

she buried her face in her hands again—"my dad's gonna kill me."

"Poor MaryEllen," I said again.

"It's worse than being the preacher's kid," she mumbled.

Mayor Stillwater appeared in the doorway. MaryEllen swallowed hard.

"Hi, Dad," she squeaked.

"Let's go, MaryEllen," he said tightly. Obviously Mayor Stillwater was controlling himself for the sake of his constituents.

"See you Monday. I hope," I whispered.

"Eeep," she said faintly.

They walked down the hall.

"G'night, Mayor Stil-*hic*-illwater," called out a cheerful, drunken voice from the overnight cells. "Nighty night-night."

Mom showed up about five minutes later, half asleep and madder than spit.

"All right," she snapped as we got into the car. "Let's have the whole thing."

My stomach lurched a little. The whole thing had started the day I climbed on a pile of desks in the furnace room and got my first good look at the ratcatcher.

She lit a cigarette and glared at me. "This had better be good."

The day Mr. Prouty told me Mom had been driving the car.

"Well?" she demanded.

"You want the whole truth?" I asked.

Mom exhaled smoke angrily. "What is it, Larch?"

I could have left things the way we had always worked it. Do not ask Mom a direct question about Dad. Do the underwear thing. But *What is it, Larch?* bent Rule Number 2 a little. Enough, maybe.

I took a deep breath and said, "Mom. I've done a bunch of wrong things, and I'm ashamed to admit it. That ever happen to you?"

Mom's cheeks turned blood-red. She knew.

She knew what I was talking about.

"Mom?"

My heart thundered in my ears. What should I do? Ask her for the truth?

"Mom. You were driving that car, weren't you? When Dad died?"

Mom leaned her head against the wheel and sighed. I was pretty sure she wasn't going to answer me. And I wondered how I could take it. The silence stretched as thin and toxic as the smoke from her cigarette.

Then, "Yep" was all she said.

Wearily she started the car. We drove around Pottsville for a while in silence, past Doc Henderson's place, and MaryEllen's house (the lights in Mayor Stillwater's study were on; poor MaryEllen), past the Duke of Donuts and out of town.

No, we did not cruise Route 62 and a particular hundred-year-old oak tree. Nothing way emotional like that. Just a road someplace. And Mom said:

"We had a fight that morning. A real big fight. That whole winter before you turned two years old, Larch, you had one earache after another. Doc Henderson said we ought to take you to see this ear specialist in Zanesville."

I kind of remembered. I had ear tubes until I was six or seven years old. In fact I lost twenty-five percent of the hearing in my left ear from all the tubes and antibiotics and stuff.

"Well. Our insurance didn't cover specialists. Your dad was complaining about the money, but I was so sick and tired of you crying every night, I didn't care about the money. I got pretty mad. I threw a pitcher of orange juice at his head."

She dragged on her cigarette. "I never told anybody that. He's got an hour to go, and I'm screaming at him. That's so evil, isn't it? But it's the truth. Funny. First time my mouth is saying it, it's telling the one person who's gonna take it personally."

You *bet* I was taking it personally. I clenched

my hands into fists. They argued, he died. I was right. No accident.

Murderer. *Murderer*.

"Well. By the time we got in the car, nobody is saying nothing to nobody. We went up Route 62, not much over the speed limit—ten, fifteen miles, maybe—when the left front tire hit a dull little patch of black ice, and the car just—slid. The steering wheel slipped out of my hands for a second. A second was all."

She threw her cigarette butt out the window and lit another. I sat, rigid, silent. Enough. I knew the truth now, right? I had heard enough. All I wanted was to get out of the car.

"Your dad grabbed my arm and said, 'Lainey!' Just once. 'Lainey!' like that. His voice was hoarse from a cold. He saw that tree coming through his window, but he didn't blame me." Mom glanced at me. "He was telling me it wasn't my fault."

She turned the car around and drove home. We were so far out in the country, hardly a house could be seen. Once in a while, the road intersected a dirt turnoff, and a feeble porch light glinted between the dark, secret trees.

"It was sweet of him, trying to forgive me like that," she said as we drove past the WELCOME TO POTTSVILLE sign. "Course, it ain't true. I know what I did." She tapped her heart. "I'm guilty as sin."

She pulled into our parking space between the trees and turned off the car. We sat staring out the windshield.

"I kept hoping," she said, "that everything would settle down to the bottom of my brain and I'd forget about it. But there you were, Larch, toddling around. Mornings, especially. You'd come into the kitchen wanting breakfast and I'd think, *Here she is—the sweet little girl you deprived of a daddy.* I closed my eyes and I prayed over and over, 'Thank you, Lord, thank you for letting my baby sleep through it, otherwise she'd curse me right now to my face.' It's why I started making doughnuts. To get away. I couldn't face the mornings anymore."

I was ready to curse her to her face, that's for sure, except I had just stumbled onto one more sick and sorry piece of the truth.

"I was in the car?" I asked.

Mom looked at me impatiently. "Strapped in the backseat. I told you, we were on our way to an ear specialist in Zanesville."

So. There was the road, slick with winter rain. And there was a woman, stunned beyond words, leaning into a car wreck and unbuckling a carseat and carrying it to the backseat of a police cruiser with a blanket draped tenderly over her baby's sleeping face to keep out the icy rain.

Then that young woman stood bare-headed in the rain watching the fire department cut through a ruined car door, standing apart as the EMTs knelt in the mess of mud and glass by the side of the car, watching her life slowly disconnect. Thinking, *That didn't happen.*

Except it did. And she had to go home and mop up orange juice off the kitchen floor. She had to reschedule her daughter's ear thing for after the funeral; had to buy a new car or fix up the wreck after the funeral. Find a job after the funeral. And drift away from church. And smoke a little more, sleep a little more, after the funeral.

Years would go by, years and years after the funeral; and waking or sleeping—

"Why didn't you tell me the truth?" I whispered.

"I just did," she whispered back.

—sleeping or waking she would push it away and push it away without a bit of forgiveness in her heart. No mercy. The rules are the rules. If you screamed at your husband, if you slammed things around, if you drove too fast, if you lost control—if you blew it so bad somebody got killed—

Well. The guilt would stick in your throat. You'd go silent. Ashamed of what you'd done and scared you'd destroy what was left.

Boy. You'd get stuck.

The tears trickled in the back of my throat. I bowed my head and gravity moved the tearflow down my nose. I stared at the tears dripping onto the backs of my hands. If my ears hadn't been so full of gunk, if Dad hadn't been a tightwad, if Mom hadn't thrown that pitcher of juice—endless, endless blame.

So weird. I smiled then. Oh, I knew why. Suddenly I was red-hot like MaryEllen, blunt like Tom Prouty. Tee-totally brave like the ratcatcher. I was unstuck, I was free, because I knew

<u>The Truth</u>

1. Jeez, Mom. I got robbed.
2. I hate it.
3. I hate you.

Awful. Ugly. But it was the truth—the part that came as natural to me as breathing, anyway. It was the other part of the truth—the hard part, the part I had to wrestle with some—that gave me the weird feeling. Like seeing the rat-catcher curled up all warm and safe and fast asleep on my bed.

And More Truth

1. I don't care anymore who was driving.
2. I love you.
3. I'm scared I'm losing you.

I looked over at Mom and took a deep, cleansing breath. I was going to tell her *The Truth*. *And* then I was going to tell her *More Truth*.

"Stupid ears," I blurted out.

Hmmm. It was a beginning, I guess. A really stupid, dumb, geeky beginning. I closed my eyes in embarrassment.

But you know what? Mom got it. Anyway, she slid her arms around me. The smoke from her cigarette drifted harmlessly out the car window while the tears on her cheeks trickled into my hair.

"Yep," she whispered.

So. We sat. We sat there together a little while, mourning my dad.

Chapter Eleven

I wanted the truth about my dad, about that car wreck nine years ago, to fit on a clean, blank piece of paper. I wanted to draw a neat line down the middle, label one column *Guilty*, the other *Innocent*, and spend the rest of my life righteous and smart and angry. But the truth ran straight off the page. Yeah, my mother was driving the day my father died. A mile to the bridge, a slick patch of ice, his voice calling out her name—and she was hurt worse than any scratch or bruise would ever show.

My mother paid, all right. She has paid and paid and paid. And for what? The truth is, Mr.

Prouty was right. That tree killed my dad.

Well. I would like to say that Mom and I grieved and forgave and found new meaning in our lives together, but that would be a lie. After five minutes of hugging in the car, we mopped our eyes, blew our noses, and went inside. Mom hit the bathroom, then closed her bedroom door and went back to sleep.

End of conversation.

The next morning, though, I sat across from Mom at the kitchen table and told her the whole messy thing about the ratcatcher and me. She didn't say a word, only shuddered when I mentioned the rat in the stove and how it brought that dog into my life with a vengeance. I told her how I hated that dog and fed it hot dogs; how I blew it at school, how I blew it at home, how I blew it with that dog. And of course, the disaster at the dog pound. Mom sighed mightily.

"Well. That dog's long gone if he's got any sense," she said. "And you're smart enough to get your schoolwork back on track. That just leaves the dog pound."

She lit a cigarette. "Maybe you and MaryEllen can offer a month's worth of cage cleaning by way of apology."

"A *month?*"

"An hour after school. That'd be twenty hours of community service. Apiece. Sounds 'bout right."

She called the Stillwaters. Monday, Mom drove MaryEllen and me to the dog pound after school.

"So after a two-hour lecture, and I say I'm sorry about a million times, and I *accept* the fact that I'm grounded until I go to college practically, your *mom* calls up and says, 'How 'bout the girls put in a little community service at the pound?' Dad loved it, of course. Why'd you do it, Mrs. Waysorta?" groaned MaryEllen. "Haven't I suffered enough?"

Mom ignored that. Mr. Prouty came out of the front entrance and said hello. I smacked my forehead. I had forgotten Mr. Prouty was also the director of the dog pound. I'd have to squeeze it into a footnote on the overdue *Who's Who* I was handing in tomorrow.

"I closed the pound for the day," said Mr. Prouty. "Not a customer in sight." He motioned for us to come in and went back to sweeping up a huge pile of dog kibble.

I about crashed into MaryEllen when she stopped dead in the doorway. Tom Prouty was leaning against the empty twenty-four-hour cage.

"*Ooooooo*, Larch," breathed MaryEllen. "My hair look okay?"

Mom slid past MaryEllen and me and looked around appreciatively. "Larch was right. This place is a wonder."

"The dog pound. Big deal," said Tom.

MaryEllen's eyes narrowed. "Excuse me?" she said. "This is not just a dog pound. This depot was the model for the whole train narrative in A.S. Hardiwick's *Stepping Off the Prairie*."

"Naw," said Tom.

"'S truth," said MaryEllen. "I read it in his biography. He stopped off for lunch in Pottsville on his way to visit his good friend—"

"—Zane Grey," said Tom reverently.

"Big deal," I said. They both ignored me. I wondered if Tom and MaryEllen would fall in love before or after they argued about every single cowboy book they'd ever read. I sure wasn't about to wait around. I strolled over to Mom and Mr. Prouty.

". . . clean some cages," Mom was saying. I rolled my eyes. Mr. Prouty rubbed his chin.

"I always thought it was a shame that the best use Pottsville could make of this fine old building was to turn it into a dog pound," he said. "It's a wonder all right, but it's a lousy pound. No outside runs for the dogs.

"So, when I heard about the—ah—jailbreak"—Mr. Prouty glanced over at me and winked—"I called Sam Balderson about his strip of land with that old turkey shed on it. We could divide the shed inside and fence individual dog runs outside. Sits on a pretty little hill. Nice shade trees. Bound to make a mean old stray downright good-natured and lovable. Might see the adoption rates go up."

"Is Mr. Balderson the one who's renovating Edward Potts's old mansion into a vegetarian retreat center?" I asked.

Mr. Prouty eyed me. "Yep," he said.

I had a brilliant idea.

"Then," I said, "then it's perfect! Swap him this building for his beat-up old turkey shed. He could renovate *this*"—I waved my arms wildly at the filthy oak molding, the furball chandelier—"and rent it out for . . ." I stopped. What *would* Pottsville do with a fabulous turn-of-the-century train depot?

"Prom night," said MaryEllen. "Weddings, definitely. Band concerts. Rotary lunches. Community sings. Breakfast with the Easter Bunny. Then there's retirement parties, and Christmas, and—"

"Meatless cook-off contests," said Mom unexpectedly. "Pack in the out-of-town vegetarians."

I stared at her. She shrugged and stuck a cigarette in her mouth.

Even Tom Prouty had an idea. "Book signings," he said. I stared at him, too. "Well, it's possible an author might come here someday and—"

"I don't know, Larch," said Mr. Prouty. "Sam's kinda strange since he gave up turkeys for vegetables. And when you come right down to it, this place is a dump. It might not appeal to him."

"It's mostly just dirty," I began, and instantly clapped my hand over my mouth.

"Larrrrrrch," moaned MaryEllen.

"Forget I said anything, Mom! Mom?"

"Hmmm," said Mom.

Which is why MaryEllen and I spent the next four weeks on our hands and knees, scraping dog hair and *worse* out of the grout between the grapevines.

Mr. Balderson went for the swap. Tom and his dad hauled the dog cages out to the turkey shed. Pretty soon Pottsville's new dog pound was filled up with stray dogs snoozing outside in the weak December sun, full of kibble and contentment. Mr. Prouty was right. Adoption rates skyrocketed.

Then came an emergency meeting of the PTO. Three days before Christmas vacation started, everybody in Pottsville sat down on folding chairs in the school gym and got the bad, bad news.

"The systemic and structural defects of Pottsville Grammar are already beyond the financial resources of the school district," said Superintendent Gordon. "Now one of the boilers has failed. We can't heat the building, and we can't afford a new furnace. So. December twenty-first will be the last day of classes at Pottsville Grammar. After Christmas break, we'll consolidate grades K through six with Blaine City. Grades seven and eight will be bused into Mount Pleasant."

My school was condemned.

What next?

"I've taken early retirement," announced Mrs. Marilyn.

MaryEllen burst into tears.

"I've accepted a lobbyist's position with Rural Ohioans for Academic Excellence," she said. "I will be lobbying the state's Department of Education for more discretionary funding for school districts in southeast-central Ohio."

She patted MaryEllen's heaving shoulder. "There, there, dear. We'll run into each other at the Duke now and then. And I guarantee you, by the end of the year, Mount Pleasant will have funding for a complete multimedia computer lab." Her eyes had a definite pig-iron gleam.

"Whoa. The Hog is back," muttered Tom Prouty.

"Those poor, poor lawmakers in Columbus," I muttered back.

It was the last great hour of Pottsville Grammar. We had cleaned out our desks and stuffed grocery bags full of forgotten art projects and broken pencils and old, D-plus history tests. We had stacked our textbooks neatly on top of the dead radiators and swept the floors.

Mrs. Marilyn warmed her hands in front of the space heater going full blast on her desk. "I have been a teacher for thirty-eight years at Pottsville," she said, "and I just now got the hang of teaching. I could teach for thirty-eight more. But if I've got to retire, I'm glad to be retiring on this class. You are all a wonder."

She glanced at the clock. "Well. We have a couple minutes left. Let's go through our Learning Teams and give the old Guiding Principles of Life one more shot. Anyone?"

Susanna Gibson raised her hand. "You can follow? Your dreams?"

"Insofar as it is possible, live at peace with one another," said John Bainter, Jr.

MaryEllen, who was still grounded, said, "Um. Don't get so carried away."

"Kindness is to do and say the kindest thing in the kindest way," announced Mindy Hardcastle.

Believe me, there was this loooong silence.

Finally Tom Prouty said, "I don't know. Zane Grey took outta Ohio and went marlin fishing and worked in Hollywood. Ronald Reagan starred in some of his movies. So I don't know. Maybe I'll write for a living."

Mrs. Marilyn looked pleased and proud. "Many best-selling authors are perfectly obnoxious people, Tom."

I kicked him under the table. "Teacher called you obnoxious," I whispered. He stuck out his tongue. I stuck out mine back.

A couple other people said stuff. When it was my turn, I stood up and said, "I guess my guiding principle is still basically The Rules Are the Rules—"

The last great dismissal bell rang. The whole

class let out a whoop and headed for the doors.

"—But," I murmured, "What Good Is Justice Without a Little Mercy?"

Nobody heard me except Tom. Tom turned and gave me a hard shrewd stare, like his imagination was outfitting me in a ten-gallon hat and horse spurs. Hmmm. Imagine someday reading about yourself in one of Tom Prouty's obnoxious best-sellers.

Ewwww.

A couple of days after Christmas, the Pottsville PTO hosted a work day at the school. Volunteers packed up the chalk and erasers and office supplies and took down the fifty-year-old wall maps. Mr. Prouty drained the last working boiler and poured antifreeze down the rows of toilets in the boys' and girls' bathrooms. Mayor Stillwater helped him board up the windows. Together they chained and padlocked the front doors. A hundred years of school. And that was that.

For the rest of seventh grade, the bus into Mount Pleasant stopped at six eighteen A.M. exactly, outside my door. My paper route got pushed earlier and earlier until I was stumbling off my bike and into the Duke about fifteen minutes after Mom got there. After a couple of months I must have looked like I needed some cheering up, because one extremely early morning just before the last day of school, Mom waited around and gave me something pretty wonderful.

"'S not my birthday," I yawned. "Is it?" I squinted at the package.

Mom rolled her eyes. "Open it, Larch."

Boy, my eyes sure popped open. I was holding in my hands an old snapshot of her and Dad standing by the river. Mom had gotten it enlarged and put into a nice wooden frame.

Frankly, I was bowled over. No way would she have given me something like that before. I hugged her twice and set the photo on the coffee table. Where it has stayed, actually. Only thing with a history to it that collects dust in our living room.

But. She had herself cropped out of the picture. All that's left of her is a couple of fingers hugging Dad's right shoulder. These days when *Fitz* comes on TV, I put my feet up on the coffee table and wrap my toes around those fingers. I ignore Lauren and her bathroom and stare at my toes instead. And I have that vision of Mom and her cigarette standing outside a dark, empty space. Now we're a step beyond the threshold where past the dark is my dad, it really is my dad, but Mom's let go of my arm somehow, let go of both arms; dead tired, exhausted from standing there alone, standing there all alone next to me.

I guess I still have plenty of crazy, mixed-up feelings about my dad. Mom doesn't talk about him much. I don't know why. The thing is, I don't let stuff like that stop me anymore. Here's what I've got so far:

My dad was born right here in Pottsville on

January 10, 1965. His best friend growing up was none other than Mrs. Marilyn's oldest son, Robbie.

"The stories I could tell about those two," said Mrs. Marilyn. Her eyes narrowed slightly.

Dad sang bass side by side with Mr. Prouty in the First Baptist choir. He ate tuna fish with mustard. He had—we had—a dog named Buster who used to growl at me. (Figures, huh?) Dad never made it to college.

And I don't know what guiding principles he followed, what rules he lived by. All I know is my dad loved me. He loved me and I miss him a lot, even though he died in a car crash before I could talk.

As for the ratcatcher—well. He's gone. I think I soured him forever on the human race. He'll go on catching rats and snarling at children until one day he gets it the other way around. Which will get him the gas for sure.

Then again, he might change a little. One day

that ugly dog might get sick and sorry and lonely for some companionship—not to mention hot dogs. He might buck up his courage and try one more time, maybe.

I admit, I pried the nails out of my bedroom window. Just in case.